ARCHIE'S WAR

Look out for more by
Margi McAllister

FAWN

Kirsty is lost, until she finds Fawn

A HOME FOR TEASEL

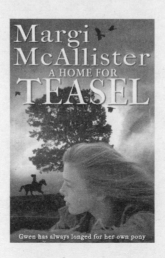

Gwen has always longed for her own pony

ARCHIE'S WAR

Margi McAllister

SCHOLASTIC

First published in the UK in 2014 by Scholastic Children's Books
An imprint of Scholastic Ltd
Euston House, 24 Eversholt Street
London, NW1 1DB, UK
Registered office: Westfield Road, Southam, Warwickshire, CV47 0RA
SCHOLASTIC and associated logos are trademarks and/or registered trademarks
of Scholastic Inc.

Text copyright © Margaret McAllister, 2014

The right of Margaret McAllister to be identified as the author
of this work has been asserted by her.

ISBN 978 1 407 14502 0

A CIP catalogue record for this book is available from the British Library.

Printed and bound by CPI Group (UK) Ltd, Croydon, CR0 4YY
Papers used by Scholastic Children's Books are made from wood grown in
sustainable forests.

1 3 5 7 9 10 8 6 4 2

This is a work of fiction. Names, characters, places, incidents and dialogues are
products of the author's imagination or are used fictitiously. Any resemblance to
actual people, living or dead, events or locales is entirely coincidental.

www.scholastic.co.uk

For Edward and William Hall
and in memory of their grandfather,
Donald Crossley

Chapter One

A rabbit ran into the walled garden and disappeared behind the apple tree. Archie ran to shut the gate but it was too late – a small dog, ears streaming behind him, was racing across the lawn after the rabbit.

Star was fast, and he loved chasing things. He darted under the bench then sprang over it, stopping for a second to sniff at a whiff of fox. But where was the rabbit? He veered round the apple tree and collided with it.

Star sat up. So did the rabbit. Alarmed, they stared at each other. Star shook his head because one of his ears had turned inside out, and sneezed. The rabbit came to its senses and ran.

Star had enjoyed the chase. He trotted back the way he had come, then stopped to inspect the stump of an old tree.

It was a great day for Star, who didn't often get into the walled garden. There were windfall plums to play with, tree stumps, and so much to sniff – a wheelbarrow, a spade, a pile of branches. He loved exploring, he loved life, and with all his heart he loved his Master Ted.

He looked up and saw that somebody had come into the garden. It was the boy who worked here. Star thought about going to meet him, but he needed to leave his mark first.

Archie shut the gate behind him. Dogs weren't supposed to be in this garden but somebody had left that gate open again and Master Ted's useless little dog was having a wee on a tree stump. That dog must be four years old by now, but most dogs had learned a bit of sense by that point. Not this one. As far as Archie could tell it didn't have half a brain from one end to the other.

"Star!" he called. "Come here, you daft thing!"

Star thought everyone was his friend so he ignored the smell of the compost heap and ran to Archie who picked him up, tucked him under one arm and set off towards the Hall. As Archie passed Gardener's Cottage, his little sister Jenn, ten years old and big enough to be helpful, appeared at the door with baby Flora on her hip.

"Tell Ma I'm taking this thing back to the Hall," he called to her. He could feel Star's tough little tail wagging against him. Master Ted thought the world of

Star, which was probably why the dog always expected something good to happen.

"I'm supposed to be helping my dad, not minding you," Archie muttered. "Gardens don't look after themselves." True, there was a team of twelve gardeners, but Bertenshaw the under-gardener wasn't much use to begin with and Archie was the head gardener's son. He had to make a good impression. At least this way he might get a chance to see Master Ted.

The quickest way to Ashlings Hall led through the kitchen garden, across the west lawn, and past the rose gardens and flower borders that Archie's dad was so proud of. Star wriggled to be down, but Archie held him more firmly so Star twisted round to lick his arm instead.

"Give over, nuisance," said Archie. Star was as silly as a box of frogs, looked like a mop and wouldn't know what to do with a rabbit if he landed on top of one. Most likely he'd hold up his paws and surrender. In the spring, when Dad had spread netting all over the vegetable garden to keep the birds off, Star had chased a cat across it. By the time they found him he was on his back and so wrapped up in netting that they'd had to cut him free with scissors. Always in the wrong place, always a nuisance. But the real trouble with Star was that he was no decent sort of dog for Master Ted. Master Ted was the son of a lord, and should have a proper grand dog.

"I said give over, you lummox," said Archie, because Star was still licking him. The other dogs at Ashlings Hall were proper dogs for the family. Lord Hazelgrove was followed everywhere by Brier the retriever, golden and splendid as a lion, and Sherlock, the enormous black Labrador. Those were real dogs, man dogs, dogs for the ruling people. Lady Hazelgrove had Connel the deerhound, a tall shaggy wolf of a beast that walked by her side like a bodyguard, her head as high as Her Ladyship's waist. A grand dog. But Star?

Nobody knew what Star's father was, but as Star was mostly white and had a square sort of face, he was probably some sort of terrier. Master Ted thought there was a bit of Westie in him.

"Bit of spaniel, too, I reckon," said Archie to the dog. "With that red-brown smudge on your head and your floppy ears. They're like a pair of curtains, are those ears. You should be a lady's dog."

Ashlings Hall was home to the Carr family, but they weren't just plain Mr and Mrs Carr. They were Lord and Lady Hazelgrove, and Archie was proud of them. The children of the Hall were all grown up now. There was Julia, the oldest and bossiest. She had married a rich Scottish lord, and now she was Lady Dunkeld. She and her husband had a Scottish castle and a house in Kent and spent most of their time there, which Archie couldn't understand. Why live in a house when you had a castle, with red deer and wildcats around? Caroline, the second eldest, was married to a diplomat and travelled all over the world. They were in Norway now, Ma said. Then there was the first son, Simon, who was something to do with the navy but seemed to spend most of his time at a desk in London.

The youngest was Master Ted. The staff should really have called him Mr Ted now that he was grown up and an officer in the army, but everyone called him Master Ted, just as everyone loved him. He cared about people. He was good at sports, friendly to all the staff, and Archie's hero. He knew every one of the families who worked for Ashlings Hall and it was Master Ted who had taught Archie and his brother to play cricket, and ride a bicycle. It was as if, when Ted appeared, you knew that very soon everyone would be having a grand time. Archie would have been happy to polish his boots. Master Ted should have had a tall faithful hound following him about, but all he wanted was a mongrel that looked like a scrubbing brush.

"No more sense than a scrubbing brush either," Archie said to Star. "You needn't think I'm going to put you down, you'll only run off again." Star was only there because somebody's poodle got over the wall and had a litter of pups. Master Ted called him "Star" after the mark on top of his head. It looked more like a smudge to Archie. But there was this to be said for Star, he was devoted to Master Ted. Followed him like a shadow. You'd think that a proper gentleman like Master Ted would be embarrassed to be followed around by a soppy-looking dog like Star. . .

Archie's freckled, wide-mouthed face opened into a grin of delight as Master Ted strode into sight. Archie put down the wriggling bundle of dog and Star galloped furiously to meet his master, wagging his tail so hard that he overbalanced, rolled, picked himself up, and hurled himself into Master Ted's arms.

"Stop licking, you soft thing!" said Master Ted, but he was laughing, turning his head away from the pink tongue as he ruffled the dog's ears. Star jumped down and darted about until he found a stone that Master Ted could throw for him, dropped it at Ted's feet, and danced a few paces backwards. Ted bowled it like a cricket ball towards the trees and Star raced after it.

"I'll get back to work then, Master Ted," said Archie, but to his joy Master Ted didn't just nod and tell him to run along. He looked down, and his kind dark eyes were smiling. Master Ted always seemed more alive than everybody else.

"Sorry about that, Archie," he said. "Has he done any damage this time?"

"No, Master Ted sir. I reckon he's just been rabbiting. Didn't catch any, sir."

"He never does. Enjoying your school holiday?"

"Very much, sir!" He had to help Dad in the gardens all summer but he liked that better than school and there was still plenty of time for climbing trees, skimming stones on the lake, and kicking a ball about with Will, his older brother.

"Tell your father from me, the gardens are looking absolutely—" he was interrupted by the ringing of a bell so strident that Archie jumped.

"Telephone," explained Master Ted. "Terrifying noise, scares the wits out of everybody. The gardens are looking absolutely splendid. Will you ask him. . ."

Archie didn't hear what Master Ted said next. Mr Grant the butler was hurrying from the house, with such a grave look on his face that something must be wrong.

"Master Ted," he said, "A telephone call from your brother, sir."

Archie turned back to the cottage, and Star followed Master Ted into the house, carrying his new favourite stone. Archie had stopped to rub greenfly off the roses when Master Ted tore past him, running as if for his life, Star at his heels.

"Archie," he shouted, turning to run backwards as he called, "I have to find my father! If you see him, if anyone sees him, he has to go back to the Hall! Immediately!" And he ran on. Archie gazed after him. Had somebody died?

When the morning's work was done Archie sat down with Will for bread and cheese in the kitchen garden. Archie was thirteen and a half but Will was eighteen months older and no longer went to school. He worked side by side with Dad. There were rules between Will and Archie, the sort of rules that are never written down but everyone understands, and they all came down to the same thing – Will was the oldest. Will was the one who had the final say about pretty much everything. He was bigger and stronger than Archie, even allowing for age – Will was big-boned and solid, and Archie would always be skinny. Will had done more and knew more. Archie had to remember that.

In return, Will guided and protected him. Will might occasionally thump Archie, but nobody else dared to lay a finger on Will Sparrow's little brother. As long as they kept to the rules, they got on very well. After the boys had eaten they were kicking a ball around under a tree when Jenn came running to meet them with her pinafore flapping about her.

"We've all got to go to the Hall!" she shouted. "Everybody on the estate, all the gardeners and keepers and everyone!"

"What for?" called Will.

"How would I know!" she said. "Ma says go home first, have a wash and put your Sunday boots on!"

Archie looked up at Will to see what he made of all this.

"Reckon somebody's died," said Will. "The Hall, and Sunday boots. Must be serious, whatever it is."

The outside staff stood awkwardly in the Great Hall at Ashlings, the men and boys with their caps tucked into their belts. The indoor servants were there, too, the maids and valets and manservants, but they were used to the grandeur of Ashlings Hall, and wore uniforms. Archie tried not to stare, but he reckoned they could fit Gardener's Cottage into the Great Hall alone. It reached up through two storeys, and had a galleried landing with doors opening from it and pillars holding up the ceiling. Opposite the front door was a wide red-carpeted staircase, the kind Cinderella might have run down with her shoe in her hand. There was a great stone hearth in one wall, but no fire in it on this warm August day. Opposite were the gleaming double doors of what somebody said was the drawing room.

Gardener's Cottage looked as if it had grown from the earth, as if tree, root and stone had worked and woven themselves into a place where a family could live comfortably like badgers in a sett. No angle of the walls was completely true, no line was perfectly straight. But the Great Hall at Ashlings was all straight lines, as far as Archie could tell. Plenty of space but too much of everything, too much polish and paint, too much carving and all those pictures on the walls in frames too big for them – and not a fingermark on anything. Archie glanced down at his hands. After all that scrubbing there was no more ingrained dirt on his hands and even his nails were clean. He wished he knew what he'd cleaned up for.

The drawing room doors opened from the inside and Grant the butler appeared. He was grey-haired with a lined face and stooped a little, but he still looked ten feet tall in his shiny shoes. Behind his back Will and Archie called him Grunt and said he was so old he had to be dug out of his coffin every morning. Today he looked so grim that it was almost funny – and in another way, not funny at all.

"Lord and Lady Hazelgrove," he announced. "And Mr Edward." Will had been right, it must be serious. Nobody ever called Master Ted "Mr Edward".

There was a soft gasp from the staff as the Hazelgroves stepped into the Great Hall. Usually, Lord

Hazelgrove wore tweeds that smelt of wet dog and tobacco. Today he was in his army uniform, the buff-coloured tunic and dark trousers of an officer in King Edward's Guards, with a row of medals over one pocket. His grey hair was neatly brushed. He had a lean face, and today looked so sad that Archie felt sorry for him.

Master Ted was in uniform, too, like a younger and slimmer version of his father. At the sight of them every man and boy in the room stood a little straighter and taller. Even beautiful Lady Hazelgrove, in a tight little buttoned-up jacket and plain skirt, looked soldierly. Connel was at her hip and the big shambling gun dogs, Brier and Sherlock, followed Lord Hazelgrove. Star pattered after Master Ted, sat down and, to Archie's disgust, scratched.

"Ladies and gentlemen of Ashlings," announced Lord Hazelgrove solemnly. "Thank you for joining us here at such short notice, and such great inconvenience. I would not lightly call you away from your work, but I have a serious announcement to make, and I wish you all to hear it together."

I wish he'd hurry up, thought Archie. *Just tell us who's died.*

"It is my sad duty to inform you," said Lord Hazelgrove, "that this country is at war with Germany."

This time it was not a soft gasp, but a sharp one. From some of the women, it was almost a shriek.

Lord Hazelgrove began to explain why they were at war but Archie, though he tried to follow, was soon confused. He understood that somebody very important had been shot in a faraway land and as a result there had been arguments between countries he'd never even heard of. But then the German king, the Kaiser, had sent his armies to take over the small country of Belgium.

"Britain has a duty to stand by Belgium," said Lord Hazelgrove, "and therefore we are at war with Germany. This will make a difference to all our lives."

Archie turned to exchange glances with Will, but Will wasn't looking at him. He stood straight as a birch tree with his head high and his eyes fixed on Lord Hazelgrove. He looked ready to march away.

"Before long," continued Lord Hazelgrove, "the army will be looking for men to go out and fight. There will be a recruiting office in the village, and men between the ages of eighteen and thirty-eight may apply. Before you all start queuing up, there are things you need to know. Lady Hazelgrove and I are proud to say that we have always taken care of you. Any of you under or over age, don't even consider going to the recruiting sergeant and lying about it. I will personally drag you back by your collars. And men with families, you can hold back."

Dad wouldn't be going, then. That was a relief.

"Some of us were around for the last business in Africa," went on Lord Hazelgrove. "War is never a good thing, but it is sometimes a necessary one. If any of you do want to join the army, your job will still be here for you when you come marching home. Your wages will be set aside for you. But I also want to say to you, if you want to join up, come and talk to me first. I'm not just your employer, I'm an old soldier too."

The back of Archie's neck itched, but he didn't dare scratch it. Lord Hazelgrove still hadn't finished.

"My son Ted will return to his regiment this week and his brother Simon is already preparing His Majesty's Navy. As for me, I'm off next week to an army training camp. They need old crocks like me to knock the recruits into shape."

Archie tried to concentrate, but the itch at the back of his neck was so bad that he was curling his toes in his boots. He thought his eyes would water or cross.

"I will be here all day for anyone who wishes to speak to me," went on Lord Hazelgrove. "Just come straight here and ask. It's that simple. Now, I'm sure you'd like some refreshment so tea, lemonade and biscuits are to be served. Ladies and gentlemen of Ashlings, three cheers for His Majesty the King!"

When the cheers had been shouted Archie finally took a good scratch at the back of his neck. A long trestle table covered with a white cloth stood beside the empty fireplace, and unsmiling housemaids bustled about with jugs of lemonade and enormous brown teapots. Some of the male staff were already lining up to talk to Lord Hazelgrove while others stood about, young footmen in suits with their hair slicked down, talking, watching each other's faces as if they were playing a guessing game. *Are you going to war? What do you think? Are you?*

"As far as I can see," said a short and muscular

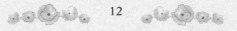

housemaid with a teapot, "it's nowt to do with us. It's all Germany this and Serbia that. Let them sort it out."

"We have to stand up for little Belgium," said Mr Grant. "If the Kaiser isn't stopped he could be in Britain this time next year, we'd have Germans running the country. Is that what you want?"

"No, Mr Grant," said the housemaid meekly, but she pulled a face behind his back as he turned away. "You two Sparrow boys, do you want lemonade?"

Archie and Will took their glasses of lemonade and sat outside in the sunshine, on the front doorstep. Ashlings had always looked so solid with all that land, the Hall and the cottages. It seemed impossible that any of it should ever change. What if Mr Grant was right, and German soldiers would take over?

"Wish I could go," said Will. "If I were old enough wild horses wouldn't stop me."

"Don't be so daft," said Archie. "You might get killed."

Will shrugged. "I can take care of myself. Soldiering's a real job. Fighting to save your country. That's a real man's job."

"So's gardening," argued Archie. He admired the way Dad could shape a tree and bring crops from bare earth.

"Do you see Master Ted gardening?" demanded Will. "In the best families like our Carrs, the lads always do soldiering. They learn it at those posh schools they go to."

"Yes, but they're officers," said Archie. "They're in

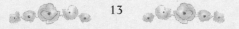

charge, they ride horses and have people to look after their kit and everything. You'd be an ordinary soldier."

"So?" said Will, and pushed his empty glass towards Archie by way of telling him to take it back to the table. Master Ted was chatting to one of Dad's assistants and looking so tall and lordly in his uniform that Archie had to stop and gaze – not for long, though, as Star made a dash for the front door and nearly knocked over a table on the way. Archie dived for him, picked him up, and headed for Master Ted. Star's tail wagged ecstatically.

"Thanks, Archie!" said Master Ted as Star reached up to lick him. "Star, I need you to look after Mother while I'm away."

Look after Mother? thought Archie. That thing couldn't look after itself. Lady Hazelgrove had Connel. All Star would do was get under her feet and Connel's big paws.

"Good luck sir," said Archie awkwardly, and added, "we'll miss you."

"Thank you, Archie, but I won't be away for long," said Master Ted cheerfully. "I'll be back for Christmas and making a nuisance of myself."

He held out his hand for Archie to shake. Archie took it and felt strong and tall with pride.

"Good man," said Master Ted. "Keep an eye on things here, won't you?" While Archie still felt six feet above the ground, Master Ted carried Star to Lady Hazelgrove.

"Star," he was saying, "you look after Her Ladyship while I'm – look at me when I'm talking to you, never

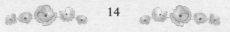

mind sniffing for biscuits. Keep her out of mischief. And no fighting."

He raised his head and spoke over the crowd to Dad. "And that goes for you too, Sparrow, if you were thinking of joining. Gardeners don't start wars, and you don't have to fight one. It should soon be over. One big punch up, and all over by Christmas."

Chapter Two

Before Dad was head gardener at Ashlings Hall, it had been Granddad. He was dead now and Dad had taken his place, but it hadn't been that simple. Bertenshaw was older and thought he should be head gardener. He was a big man with a lump of a head and bristles on his face and arms. He scowled all the time and never spoke to any of Archie's family if he could help it. He even scowled at baby Flora.

"Walter Sparrow only got that job because of his father," grumbled Bertenshaw. But everyone on the estate knew that Bertenshaw was lazy and only did as much work as he really must. Archie's Dad loved the gardens almost as much as he loved his own family. He didn't make a fuss about it. Watching the neat, precise way he pruned a rose bush or pressed seedlings into the earth was like watching a musician. Dad wouldn't let Bertenshaw prune roses. He was too careless, and too rough with them.

Dad had a way of teaching Will and Archie how to understand what the plants needed. "What's it trying to tell you?" he would say if a tree was wilting or a bud failed to flower. When he'd been tiny, Archie had thought that the plants could talk and for some reason he couldn't hear what they said. When he was older, he understood what Dad meant. Brown leaves or pinched buds were a tree's way of telling you something was wrong. It was thirsty, or in the wrong place, or something was attacking its roots. All the other gardeners respected Dad and had no time for Bertenshaw. The morning after war was declared, Bertenshaw trudged past Gardener's Cottage with a sneer, as if the war was all Dad's fault.

Ma had grown up at Ashlings, too. Her father had farmed one of Lord Hazelgrove's farms.

"Lady Hazelgrove still looks beautiful," she was saying, the morning after war was declared. "I was watching her in the Great Hall yesterday, she's as lovely as she was the day she was married, and more elegant now she's older, and she walks like a queen."

"I remember that wedding," said Dad. "It was the biggest thing in the village for years. We all got a half-day holiday, and the children got sixpence. I were eleven year old, but I helped my Pa with the flowers. His Lordship wanted an arch of roses over the door and we did it, too. We were right proud of that."

"At school we had to make a banner with their names on, Charles and Beatrice," said Ma. "I designed a monogram and I thought it was beautiful, but I did it with C, B, and H, because I thought their surname was Hazelgrove. You would think so, wouldn't you? I did this beautiful design and showed it to my teacher, and she said, 'Don't you know their name is Carr? Have you lived in this village all your life and you don't know the name of the people at the Hall? His Lordship's title is Lord Hazelgrove. His surname is Carr.' And she went on and on about it, until I cried."

"She was a nasty old broomstick," said Dad. "I hated her."

"I reckon she thought Lady Hazelgrove wasn't good enough," said Ma. "A lot of the women were like that."

"Lady Hazelgrove not good enough!" repeated Archie.

"She wasn't from one of the old families," said Ma. "Her grandfather was an engineer who made whole mints full of money building railway engines. So the village said that she wasn't a real lady, just a rich girl, but she looked and talked like a lady."

"They all like her now," said Archie.

"She spent her money wisely," said Ma. "She got cottages repaired, she had water taps put in houses, she put up the money to pay the doctor's bills for them that couldn't afford them. And she made that horrible teacher retire, so the children all loved her. She was a sensible woman. She earned respect."

"It's the best way," said Dad. "Respect should be

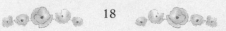

earned. Now Archie, go and pick the peas and beans for the Hall and carry them up to the kitchen. And half a dozen lettuces, and find out if they want raspberries today."

It was one of the jobs that had to be done every day, picking the fresh fruit and vegetables and carrying them to the Hall. Archie took a trug to the garden and picked the long green beans. *War*. It sounded exciting until you realized that people would really be shooting each other. *Shooting at Master Ted*. But Master Ted would come through anything. He had to, because life wouldn't be the same without him.

In a cloud of white, Star careered through the garden. That dog was never where it was meant to be. He stopped suddenly at a row of cabbages and pushed his nose into the leaves.

"Star!" shouted Archie. The dog stopped and looked up, wagging his tail and looking hopeful.

"Where's Ted?" called Archie, hoping that Star would look for his master instead of weeing on the cabbages. "Find Ted!" From a long way off came two short sharp whistles, and Star whirled round and dashed off towards the Hall. The kitchen garden was another place where gates were meant to be kept shut, but Star was small enough to wriggle underneath them. Couldn't he be kept on a lead?

Archie lifted the trug, which was heavy now. He only went to the Hall to deliver fruit and vegetables to the kitchen, but he'd occasionally glimpsed the way the family lived. He didn't envy all that ceremony. At

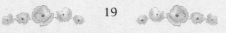

Gardener's Cottage they ate from earthenware plates on weekdays and Ma's blue and white willow pattern on Sundays, and sat around a scrubbed wooden table with a cloth on it. He and Will shared a bed, and always had. Little Flora had a cot in Dad and Ma's bedroom, but when she was bigger she'd sleep in the attic with Jenn. The bath hung up against the back wall of the house, to be put in front of the fire on bath nights. Ma thought their cottage was heaven. They had taps in the house, and a stove that heated water. What more did they need?

At the Hall the family ate in a room bigger than their whole cottage, with silver on a table that shone like water. You wouldn't dare spill anything. There was a room the size of the village school for sitting around in and another one just for a library, their *own* library. And everyone had their own bedroom along miles of corridors. Did they not get lost going to bed? Even Lord and Lady Hazelgrove had rooms of their own, and Ma said they had feather beds, too. Ma said that Lord and Lady Hazelgrove had little rooms for getting dressed in. Archie couldn't understand why they needed them, but he was proud of the Carrs of Ashlings. They lived in style. The peas and beans in the silver dishes? The strawberries to eat with cream? *We grew those. My Dad and Will and me, we grew those.* And the best of the Carrs of Ashlings was Master Ted, who knew every child on the estate by name and had time to listen to everyone. Star might be more trouble than he was worth, but he knew a good master when he saw one.

Master Ted had always got on with everyone on the estate. He'd play cricket and footie with the village kids. He used to take Will and Archie fishing and he'd taught them to bowl overarm, too. Every year on Midsummer Day, the longest day of the year, he led the Hall team in the Hall versus Village Dawn to Dusk Cricket Match, which began at sunrise and ended at sunset. There was no limit to the numbers on the teams, so almost all the men and boys in the village took part and tea was served from a marquee on the lawn. That summer, Archie's proudest moments had been when he batted on Master Ted's team.

In winter Ted joined in with snowball fights and sledging. One bitter morning three years ago, when Archie had been carrying vegetables to the house, he'd slipped on the ice and hurt his foot so badly that he couldn't walk, but Master Ted had seen him, scooped him up, and carried him back to the cottage where they'd all sat drinking tea at Ma's table, Archie with his bandaged foot up on a chair. They'd eaten freshly baked lardy cakes, and Master Ted had licked the stickiness from his fingers and said it was much nicer than the cakes they got at the hall.

"There's no side to Master Ted," Ma had remarked later. "He gets on with anyone, and that's the sign of a real gentleman."

Now, from the back door of the Hall, Archie made his way to the Servants' Hall, which smelt of soap and boiled cabbage. Aggie the big bony kitchenmaid was there and Archie gave her the basket.

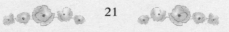

"I suppose you'll be off for a soldier, Archie Sparrow," she said.

"He's not old enough," said the cook firmly. "And when he's old enough, it'll be over."

"Hey up!" said Will next day, coming back from the village. "The army's arrived!"

Archie looked over his shoulder, half expecting to see troopers in the kitchen doorway. Will laughed.

"Not here, you soft lummox. In village. In t'church hall."

The soldiers had set up a long table in the church hall, he said, and senior soldiers – the recruiting sergeants – sat behind them. Any man old enough and fit enough to fight could sign up there.

"Oh, yes?" said Ma. "They'll have a lad in a uniform before he can say, 'Which way's France?'"

"Sam Hardy tried to join," Will told them.

"Sam the Boots?" said Archie. Sam was the boy who cleaned the boots and did other odd jobs at the Hall. He and Archie had known each other all their lives.

"Sam was standing up tall and swearing he was eighteen," said Will. "But his Uncle David was in the queue to sign up too, and he told the officer the truth about how old Sam was, and then he got Sam's granny, 'cause she lives across the road, and Granny Hardy barged in like storm and fury. She gave the sergeant an earful and dragged Sam back by his coat collar, marched him all the way back to the Hall."

"How do you. . ." began Archie, but Will gave him a

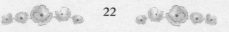

look that silenced him. Presently Ma left the room, and Archie felt it was safe now to ask the question.

"How do you know what went on at the recruiting office?"

"Everyone's talking about it," Will told him. "The first lot are marching off on Friday morning. I reckon Dad might let us go and watch. Give them a good send-off."

"When's Master Ted going?" asked Archie.

"Same time as the rest of them, eleven," said Will. "He's leading them off."

Chapter Three

Archie woke early and couldn't get back to sleep so he pulled on his clothes, slipped quietly outside, and walked slowly and thoughtfully through the gardens. *Gardeners don't start wars.* Master Ted had said that, and the words had repeated in Archie's head as he lay in bed. Master Ted didn't start wars either, but he had to go and fight in one.

In the autumn Dad had cut down an old cherry tree. It had been a grand old tree but it had withered and failed at last, and now the wood was stacked in the shelter of a wall. Archie and Will were allowed to help themselves to the small pieces and Archie, picking through them, found a short, thick piece of branch. He took it home and sat on the doorstep, paring at it with his penknife as the shavings curled to the ground.

He was fond of this penknife, which had been his present from the Carr family the previous Christmas. He was pretty certain that Master Ted had chosen it for him. Dad had showed him and Will how to carve simple animals and he'd intended to make a dog but the wood was all the wrong size and shape for a dog, so he sat scraping the blade steadily down the grain, waiting to see how it turned out. It seemed that even when a tree was cut down, it could tell you what it wanted. By the time he'd shaped it a bit more he thought it would make a good sword – a very small one, not much bigger than his hand, but still a sword – and turned it the other way to shape the hilt. He was still there when the smell of frying bacon wafted past him through the open door and made his stomach yearn with hunger. Dad came to the door and watched what Archie was doing.

"Nice piece of work, is that," commented Dad.

"It's for Master Ted," said Archie. He'd only just thought of that, and realized he wanted to give Master Ted something he'd made himself. Until now it had just been a bit of wood to whittle, but now that it was a present for Master Ted it was precious. By breakfast time he had finished it, taking care with every stroke of the blade, and sandpapered it smooth. Finally, he turned it in his hands to inspect it. It needed a finishing touch.

"Has Master Ted got any middle names?" he asked.

"Your Ma would know," said Dad.

"Francis Stephenson," called Ma from the house.

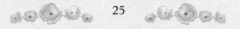

"Edward, then Francis, after his Uncle Francis, and Stephenson from Her Ladyship's side."

Everyone was in a good mood at breakfast time. The hens were laying well so there were plenty of eggs, and Flora soon had buttercup yellow streaks of yolk across her face. Jenn tried to clean it off but Flora didn't want to be cleaned, and screwed up her face. She looked like a cross kitten.

"Dad," said Archie, "may I go the village to see the men march off? They're leaving at eleven from outside the church."

"Me too?" asked Will with a mouthful of bacon.

"Manners, our Will!" said Ma sternly.

"Can I too?" pleaded Jenn. "I'll take Flora, Ma, so she won't be under your feet."

"You can all go," said Dad. "Give them a send-off."

"Aye, if they must fight wars they may as well have something to smile about when they march away," said Ma. "They won't be smiling when they get to France, or Belgium, or wherever they get to."

When Will and Archie put on their jackets to go to the village Ma was packing bundles into two willow baskets. Archie took the wooden sword from his pocket and began to carve "EFSC" into the hilt. Then he sandpapered it again, because it had to be perfect for Master Ted.

"There's some Ashlings roses for the lads," said Ma, her back turned to them as she bent over the baskets. "White roses for Yorkshire and sweet pinks, and I've put paper and pins in there, too, they'll need pins."

"Ma!" exclaimed Will in horror. "Soldiers don't want flowers!"

Ma whirled round with such a glare that they both stepped back and ducked. Her hands were on her hips.

"And what do you know, Master William Sparrow, all of fifteen years old, what do you know about what soldiers want?" She banged the basket on to the kitchen table so hard that petals drifted to the floor. "You don't know you're born! My cousins all fought in South Africa and I know a bit more about the world than you do." Then she paused, and the fight seemed to go out of her. "I've known Master Ted since he were a littlie, and most of those lads, too. Off you go, now, and give them a cheer."

It's a good thing our Jenn's going, thought Archie. *She won't mind carrying flowers.*

The head gardener's family weren't the only ones walking to Ashlings village that morning. On the way they met with other families who worked for the Carrs, the carpenter and his daughters and the gamekeeper's wife and children, and when they reached the church everything was as crowded and busy as a market day. A little crowd stood at the door of the Fox and Geese public house. Everybody seemed to have brought something for the soldiers, mostly photographs or little bags of sweets, so Archie was glad to have something to give even if it was flowers. He was even more glad to have the little wooden sword. Ever since that moment of understanding that it was for Master Ted, he had looked forward to putting it into his hand.

27

Now, wherever Master Ted went, the sword would go too.

Archie looked round for Master Ted and couldn't see him anywhere. A tall young lad stood still for his mother to tuck a prayer book into the top pocket of his tunic. A pretty girl slipped something into a soldier's hand. Lord and Lady Hazelgrove stood beside the car where Star and the chauffeur still sat, and Archie guessed that they had already said goodbye to Master Ted privately. Lords and ladies didn't do crying and hugs in public. The coalman was there, a couple of teachers from the grammar school in town, and Frank Roger who sang in the church choir. All the girls fancied Frank Roger.

"They have to march to the train at Kirby Moss," said Will, who'd been talking to some men in uniform. "Then they get the train to the camps."

"What camps?"

"Where they train to be proper soldiers, daftie. They don't go straight off to war."

The door of the village hall opened and a cheer went up – there was Master Ted in his officer's uniform, shoes and belt gleaming, a glowing smile on his face and a sword at his side like a prince. Then Star jumped from the car, raced through the crowd, and leapt into his arms. By the time Master Ted had fussed him and put him down, a mist of white hairs coated the smart uniform. Star ran twice round him and once round Will, then put his paws up at Archie, who ignored him. That dog was excited enough without encouraging him.

"My ma sent these, sir," he said, ushering Jenn

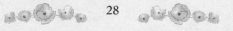

forward with the basket and hoping that they didn't look like flower sellers.

"What a nice woman your mother is!" exclaimed Master Ted. "Flowers from Ashlings!" He fastened a white rose to his tunic. "Just the thing! Thank her very much for me!" He raised his voice. "Chaps, we have roses and pinks from Ashlings to see us on our way! Anyone for a white rose?"

The men gathered round, and suddenly Archie and Jenn were so busy handing out flowers that he almost forgot the wooden sword in his pocket. It was only when he caught sight of Master Ted's sword hilt that he remembered it and drew it out, but he hadn't got hold of it properly and somebody jolted him. The sword dropped from his hand and disappeared among the men's boots, and before Archie could find it Star had darted forward. The dog snatched up the sword, ran to the shade of a chestnut tree and settled down to chew.

"Star!" bellowed Archie, forgetting that he shouldn't shout at Master Ted's dog, especially in front of all these people. Desperate to get it back before Star could gnaw it to splinters he ran, but Star saw him and sensed a good game. He picked up the sword and galloped across the churchyard and out of sight.

The men had seen and were laughing, and there was nothing Archie could do. He stared hard at the churchyard wall, burning with embarrassment, forcing hot tears back from his eyes. He liked dogs. He could never be unkind to one. But for those seconds, he hated Star.

From behind him somebody whistled twice. Master Ted's clear, strong voice rang out.

"Star! Star, *give!*"

To the cheers of the men Star whisked round and flew back to Master Ted with his ears streaming behind him. He dropped his prize at Ted's feet and sat back, watching with big bright eyes.

"What have you got, Star?" said Master Ted. "Sorry about that, Archie. This is yours, I believe."

"It was meant for you, sir," muttered Archie wretchedly, but now everything was ruined and wrong and he felt ridiculous. He took the sword, wet with dog spit and pitted with tooth marks, wiped it on his arm, and offered it back. "It's supposed to be for luck, sir."

Master Ted turned the sword slowly in his hands. "It's even got my initials on it!" he exclaimed, and Archie's heart lifted a little. Master Ted looked like a small boy with a new boat. "Archie, did you make this yourself?"

"Yes, Master Ted sir. It's wood from the old cherry tree, sir."

Master Ted seemed to be gazing at something far away. Then he put his hand on Archie's shoulder and smiled down.

"That's the most perfect thing anyone's given me today," he said. "Thank you, Archie. Made just for me with my initials, and our old cherry tree too. It's like having a bit of Ashlings to take with me everywhere I go. And since Star got hold of it – no, you menace, you're not getting it back – it's even got his tooth marks, so it's something of him, too."

"Good luck, sir," said Archie. Then somebody shouted and the men in uniform began to line up, Master Ted took Star to Lady Hazelgrove, then strode to the front of the column.

"Ashlings men!" he shouted. "Finish saying goodbye to your sweethearts. All of them, Frank Roger! We've got a war to fight! Attention!"

There was a stamping of boots. The sergeant barked an order, then they were marching away as if they would follow Master Ted to the edge of glory, further and further away, out of the village, and Archie found he was longing for them to stop, please stop, all of you, come back, come home, because roses and wooden swords wouldn't keep them safe. . .

Will was staring after the men with envy and yearning. Lord Hazelgrove's car growled into life.

"Got any money?" said Will at last. They had enough between them for a quarter of peppermints to share with Jenn and Flora. They walked home thinking of what they had seen, and saying very little.

In the evening Star trotted restlessly about the Hall, looking for Master Ted. He padded steadily from room to room but Master Ted wasn't in any of the downstairs rooms, so Star tried his bedroom. Even there he couldn't find Ted, but at least there was a comforting smell of him in his old shoes. In his bathroom there was a towel that smelt of him. Star's basket was in a corner of Master Ted's bedroom. He knew that sometimes Master Ted went away for night after night, and this might be one of those times, so he trotted about looking for things that smelt of Master Ted.

"I'm afraid Master Ted's dog has taken the towel from the small bathroom to his basket, my lady," said Mrs Satterthwaite the housekeeper. "The maid tried to take it away, but he growled, so she thought best to leave it."

"She can leave it there," said Lady Hazelgrove. "But we'll bring the basket downstairs. There's no point in him sleeping in Ted's room when Ted's not there." But when they tried to move the basket Star showed his teeth and cowered down with his old blanket and Master Ted's towel.

"If that's the way he feels, he can stay in here," said Lady Hazelgrove, so Star's basket remained in Master Ted's bedroom. The next night he took Master Ted's shoes to bed with him because he liked the familiar smell of his feet. He took his wooden-handled clothes brush in there, too, for safekeeping and for something to chew.

"That dog," muttered Mr Grant. "It'll take anything that's not nailed down."

Day by day Star discovered that he could survive without Master Ted, but he missed him terribly. Ted's mother was kind, but he and Ted belonged to each other. Life wasn't so much fun without him.

Archie went into the potting shed and chalked lines beneath a shelf on the back wall. A line for every day Master Ted had been away, in blocks of seven. There were two, then three, then four.

When Archie walked back from trips to the village he would see Star at a window, gazing along the drive. On warm days the dog would sit outside on the steps or he'd be lying down because he had waited so long and was tired. Star no longer tore round the gardens getting under everyone's feet, but Archie realized it was better when he did. He missed Star. Once he sat down on the steps beside him to stroke him and talk to him, but then Mr Grant had told him off because the garden boys weren't supposed to be seen at the front of the house.

After that Archie waited for the next Thursday, because Thursday was Mr Grant's day off. With Grant safely out of the way, Archie slipped round to the front of the hall with a few leftover crumbs of toffee in his pocket. Star was lying with his head on his paws as if he knew that Master Ted wasn't coming today, but he may as well wait anyway.

"Hello, you," said Archie. He sat down beside Star and offered him the toffee from his fingers. Star sniffed cautiously, then settled his head down again.

"Hey," said Archie softly. "It's nice. Go on. Haven't you even enough sense to lick toffee? Do you want some company? I'll sit here with you a bit. Grunt isn't going to chase me away, not today." Star began to lick his fingers, hesitantly at first, then with enthusiasm, and Archie smiled. It wasn't Star's fault that he was such a riot of a dog. And he was loyal to Master Ted.

"I know, you miss him," he said, stroking Star's head. "We all do. He'll come back."

*

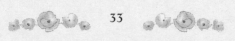

The war came close to Yorkshire. Gunboats fired at Scarborough, and a local lad was wounded in action. They had said it would be over by Christmas. The days grew shorter. Autumn leaves fell until the trees were bare and only the evergreens stayed, rising above morning frost. With every line on the potting shed wall Christmas drew nearer, and the war still went on.

Archie wanted Christmas to be as it always was. Everybody else on the estate seemed to think so too, including Lady Hazelgrove, so Archie and Will dragged bundles of holly and ivy through the gardens to decorate the Hall, and climbed trees to cut mistletoe. There were leeks and carrots to be dug, and the kitchens at the Hall smelt of spice and brandy. When he delivered the vegetables, Cook would slip him a mince pie or a piece of shortbread.

Lord Hazelgrove came home for Christmas, smiling broadly and striding out like the old soldier he was. Simon, the older son, would be coming, but nobody knew about Master Ted. Ted's sister Lady Dunkeld arrived, giving orders to everyone and annoying the cook. Archie found that he was watching and waiting all the time, hoping that he would go to the kitchens and find everyone happy and excited and saying "Master Ted's home!" But there was no news of Master Ted, and he felt more and more sorry for Star. He still stopped to talk to the dog and give him a bit of fuss if he was on the step, and if Grant wasn't looking. In the harsh cold of December Star was more often indoors at the window, but Archie saw him trotting round the grounds when Lady Hazelgrove or one of the household staff took him for walks. He only trotted now, never galloped.

Two days before Christmas Archie trailed home from the village with some shopping for Ma. He was nearly at the Hall when he heard Star barking as he had never barked in his life, as if not a hundred million barks could be loud enough for the joy, joy, joy. . .

It could mean only one thing. Master Ted was home!

"Thank you," said Archie. He didn't exactly know who he was thanking, but he had to thank someone.

Chapter Four

At Gardener's Cottage there were presents, oranges, nuts, and a Christmas pudding sent from the Hall and boiled up in the steamy kitchen, but best of all, Master Ted was home with not so much as a bruise as far as anyone could tell. On Boxing Day all the staff visited the Hall and were given presents by the family – proper tweed caps for Will and Archie – and Ted whispered to Archie that his sword was still safe. It was his lucky charm, he said.

Archie had almost forgotten what Star was like when Ted was there. It was as if a spell had been lifted from him and he brimmed with life. His tail wagged, his eyes were bright, he was under everyone's feet again, and it was as if he had never been so happy. But Master Ted was different. His smile wasn't the same, and he looked older. If Lord Hazelgrove took friends shooting, Master Ted didn't go with them. At the sound of a gunshot he would look sharply round with a tense, focused expression. But even though it was winter he found time for a bit of cricketing practice with Will, Archie and Sam the Boots. Star would tear round the lawn to find the ball.

"Do you think Master Ted's changed?" Archie asked Will as they left the Hall.

"Course he has," said Will. "He's been in a war and he knows he has to go back soon. He must have seen men die and everything. If they'd only let me join the army I could go and keep an eye on him."

Master Ted wouldn't be home for long, but he found time for the gardens. There was some neglected land not far from the house where Dad wanted to make a sunken garden with ferns and a pond. Archie went with them to look at the site, mostly so he could be with Master Ted, but he had another reason. He wanted to make himself extremely useful in the Christmas holiday because then Dad might take him on full time, just like Will, and he wouldn't have to go back to school in January. They were coming round the corner of the house with Master Ted and Dad striding along in step, and Star stopping to water every blade of grass, when they heard the roar, clunk and cough of an engine.

"Car coming," said Dad. Star was barking furiously, so Archie grabbed him and hung on.

"Pardon me, Master Ted sir," he said, "but he'd likely get run over."

"He hasn't a clue about cars," said Master Ted. "He loves being in them, but from the outside he thinks they're dragons. My word! It's Betters!"

"Betters?" Dad mouthed the word at Archie, but he didn't know what it meant, either. Master Ted broke into a run as the car stopped and a young man with a curling moustache jumped down from the driving seat.

"Betters!" cried Master Ted. "Good to see you!"

The newcomer slapped Master Ted on the back and looked past him at Archie. He winked, and called out.

"I'm looking for Captain Carr! Seen a Captain Carr anywhere?"

Archie was about to say "no", then with a gasp he understood.

"Master Ted, sir!" he exclaimed.

"That's *'Captain* Master Ted, sir'!" said the stranger, and extended his hand to shake. "Captain Arthur Bettany, making a nuisance of myself. Ted and I survived school together and France, too, somehow." He turned back to Master Ted. "Sorry I couldn't let anyone know I was coming, I just got away and thought you'd like to know about your promotion."

"Many congratulations, Master Ted, sir," said Dad.

"Oh, you know how it is," said Master Ted and shrugged, and Archie thought he looked embarrassed. "Promotion comes quickly in wartime."

It turned out that Captain Bettany – "Betters" – was an old friend of Master Ted, and they had been stationed near to each other in France, or "at the Front" as the soldiers called it. Master Ted seemed happier

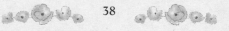

with his friend around and Archie liked Captain Bettany. Soon they were organizing games of football between the estate workers and the indoor servants with Master Ted on one side and Captain Bettany on the other, which meant that they fouled each other at every chance they had. Star joined in until Archie was convinced that the dog's only aim in life was to trip people up. Now and again Star ran into the gardens and had to be summoned out by Master Ted's whistle. Bertenshaw glowered at them.

"We don't want Star digging everything up, the menace," said Master Ted. "Archie, it'll help if you learn my whistle for when I'm not here."

After a lot of practise Archie managed to do the short, sharp double whistle that Master Ted used for calling Star. He did it so well that Star would spin round in the middle of a run, charge up to him, realize who it was and wheel off again to find Master Ted. It made Flora shriek with laughter. Star was trouble, but he was fun.

The Christmas break was passing too quickly, and now it was three days, now two . . . then Archie took the vegetables to the Servants' Hall and smelt metal polish. They were getting Ted's kit ready for him to go.

It seemed all wrong. He'd only just come back.

"What's up with you?" Will said when Archie trudged back to the cottage.

"Master Ted's off int' morning," he said. "When he got his promotion, he said 'promotion comes quickly in wartime'. What did that mean?"

"Dead men's shoes," said Will promptly. "It means stepping into dead men's shoes. You get promoted because some other poor beggar's been shot."

Archie wished he didn't know that. Star was always under everyone's feet – couldn't he just trip Master Ted up so that he broke his leg and couldn't go back? *He's our Master Ted*, thought Archie.

Star nearly did trip up Master Ted that night because he was anxious about him, and wanted to stay as close as he could. Ted's uniform was laid out for the morning and Star didn't like that uniform. When Ted wore that, he went away. There was a nasty smell of polish, too. Star tried chewing a leather belt but whatever was in that polish, it tasted foul. Ted's boots were gleaming, too. Star took one and hid it under the bed, but Ted found it.

Early the next morning, Archie was carrying the vegetable basket to the Hall when he heard the roar of a car engine. Master Ted and Captain Bettany were returning to war. On his way back, Archie slipped round to the front of the house. Star was lying on the step with his head on his paws.

"Poor little beggar," said Archie. "You'll be cold." He was about to go and hug some warmth into the dog, hoping he wouldn't be in trouble with Mr Grant again – but Lady Hazelgrove came to the door, picked Star up, and carried him back into the Hall, stroking and soothing him. Once again, Star and Lady Hazelgrove were to look after each other.

*

After Master Ted and Captain Bettany had gone away, Dad and Will were sent for, to come to the Hall. Will came out with his whole face bright, and broke into a run when he saw Archie. "I'm going to Kent!" he shouted.

"What?" asked Archie.

"If Ma says yes, but she will. Kent, dimmie, wake up. You know Master Ted's sister, Miss Julia that was. . ."

"Lady Dunkeld, of course I know."

"Well, her gardeners keep trooping off and enlisting, see, and they need a new garden lad. She wants me to go!"

Gardeners didn't start wars, Master Ted had said. But Archie was finding that they went to fight in them, all the same.

"You're already training with Dad!" he said.

"Yes, but if I go to Kent I can learn stuff I won't learn here. It's warmer, they can grow things that won't grow in Yorkshire. The growing season starts in March, *March*, and right through into the autumn. And it leaves the way open for you, doesn't it? If I go to Kent, you'll be the one working with Dad."

"Won't you miss home?"

Will shrugged. "I'll be fine. I'll be back for holidays."

Archie felt glad it was Will, not him. He couldn't have left home so easily.

"It'll just be me and the lasses at home now," he said. "It's better with you."

"You'll be all right," said Will. "You can leave school. You'll be a real gardener."

41

Ma didn't want Will to go, and had some sharp words to say about the war that had caused it. He was too young, she insisted, he was needed at home, Archie shouldn't be leaving school yet. But Lady Dunkeld always got what she wanted, and next time Lady Hazelgrove went to Kent, Will and his trunk went with them. Will was restless with excitement.

"I'll go in a car to the station!" he said. "Then on a train! And Lady Dunkeld's chauffeur's going to pick us up and take us to her house!"

"It's not just Lady Dunkeld that's short of staff," remarked Dad drily. "There's men leaving here all the time to join up. Bertenshaw can just do some real work for a change."

When Will had gone two of Dad's assistants joined the army, saying that at least it would be warmer in France. It would be a grim winter. Archie cleaned pots and filled seed trays when his fingers were clumsy with cold, and dark came early. He began another series of chalk marks on the potting shed wall. Bertenshaw, complaining of his bad back and his cough, found fault with everything Archie did. He trudged round with his big shovel-shaped head huddled into his shoulders.

Archie learned to keep out of Bertenshaw's way as much as he could, but there were times when they had to work together preparing vegetable beds. One chilly winter afternoon when Archie was sick of the sight of the vegetable bed, the light was fading and it was almost time to go home and get warm, Star trotted to the garden gate, stood on his hind legs, and pushed it open.

"Hello, you!" said Archie. Star turning up was the best thing that had happened all afternoon.

"You left that gate unlocked," growled Bertenshaw. Archie knew that it was Bertenshaw's mistake, not his, but it was no use saying so. He left his spade in the ground and went to greet Star, who trotted to meet him.

Something flew through the air past him. A stone crashed on to the path where Star had just been.

"What are you doing?" Archie dashed to Star, bundled up the dog in his arms, and turned to yell at Bertenshaw. "Don't you ever do that! Don't ever throw stones at a dog!"

Bertenshaw strode towards them. Archie stood his ground, but he held Star, who was growling, more closely.

"And don't you raise your voice to me, you insolent brat!" he ordered. "If you weren't the boss's son you'd be out of a job for that!" As Archie turned away, he yelled, "and don't you turn your back on me!"

"I'm taking the dog back to the Hall," said Archie, carrying Star out of the garden.

"Going to tell tales to Her Ladyship, then?" snarled Bertenshaw.

But Archie didn't tell anyone about it. He just made sure to check gates after that, and tried to ignore Bertenshaw. Most people did. Even Bertenshaw's own two sons ignored him. They didn't live with him, and never wrote. Long ago, Mrs Bertenshaw had run away

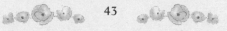

back to her mother, taking the two boys with her to save them from his fists. None of them ever came to see him.

Will wrote occasionally, saying how much further on the gardens were in Kent. Everything seemed to grow two weeks earlier, he said. At Ashlings, Flora had colds all winter. Ma and Jenn knitted scarves and mitts for soldiers.

When snow fell Archie and Jenn had a snowball fight but it wasn't so much fun without Will and Master Ted around, and soon there was nothing but sheets of black ice. Dad instructed Bertenshaw to spread grit over the paths.

"Can't the lad do it?" complained Bertenshaw.

"I'm telling you to do it," said Dad.

"It's a lad's job, is that," grumbled Bertenshaw, but Dad ignored him.

In the Hall, Star pined. He would sniff about looking for Ted, then sigh deeply and take up his place at the window again. He curled up at night in a nest of Ted's old clothes as if they could keep each other warm. He had finally managed to find a boot, and took that to bed too. Food didn't taste the way it did when Ted looked after him, except if it was liver or chicken, something he liked very much. Her Ladyship fed him well and was kind, but he only wanted Ted to come home.

The next morning Aggie the kitchenmaid came picking her way cautiously across the frozen grass, her nose pink with cold. Lady Hazelgrove would like snowdrops, she said, to decorate the house. Dad nodded at Archie.

"Away you go, son," he said. Archie ran across the snowy grass to the sheltered corner where snowdrops grew in drifts, hoping that Bertenshaw wasn't about. He could imagine what he'd say – "Picking flowers now? That's a girl's job" – but Bertenshaw was a long way off tying strings over the delicate yellow crocuses to keep the birds from eating them. In the distance Lady Hazelgrove was walking Connel, but Star had wandered off and was getting dangerously close to Bertenshaw. Archie gave the two short sharp whistles Master Ted had taught him.

As soon as he'd done it he hated himself. At the sound of that whistle Star turned, his ears twitched up, and happiness shone in his eyes. He bounded across the lawn, bolted straight past Archie and round the corner of the nearest hedge, then emerged again more slowly, puzzled and searching.

"Star, come here!" called Archie, but Star wasn't interested and Archie couldn't bear to watch him looking for Master Ted. Hurting with regret he turned away and bent his head over the snowdrops. By the time he had cut enough of the thin green stems to make a bunch, Lady Hazelgrove and Connel were on their way to find Star.

"Good morning, my lady," said Archie, touching his cap.

Star was puzzled. He knew he'd heard a whistle, but he'd searched everywhere without even a whiff of Ted's

boots. He pattered slowly back to the safety of Connel and Ladyship, but was distracted by a sack lying on the path. Curiosity was too much for him, and he pushed his nose into it.

Toys! thought Star. *A bag full of toys!* He sniffed about and chose his favourite one.

"Star!" shouted Archie. "No!", then he turned hot, and his legs weakened. For the second time, he'd shouted at Star in front of the family. Star turned to face him, his eyes wide and a large potato wedged in his mouth.

"Beg pardon, my lady," he said. "I was afraid he might have got hold of a bulb, and some of them are poisonous. But it's just a sp . . . a potato, my lady."

"Star, give," ordered Lady Hazelgrove. Star dropped the potato at her feet and sat back.

"Now he wants me to throw it," she sighed. "Will you do it, Archie? I'm sure your arm is stronger than mine."

Archie threw the potato, and Star's ears flapped as he ran after it. He looked thinner than he used to.

"It's so good to see him enjoying something," said Lady Hazelgrove. "He misses Ted so much, he's even off his food." She lowered her voice. "I can't even say Ted's name in front of him. He goes looking for him."

Archie hoped she hadn't heard that stupid whistle. He turned red just thinking about it. Star brought the potato back. He threw it again and, still red, dared to suggest an idea.

"I could take him for walks if you like, my lady," he said.

"Thank you," she replied, but there was something

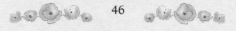

final about her voice that told him the answer would be "no". "That's most kind of you, Archie, but there's no need. Star and I look after each other." Neatly, she changed the subject. "We had a letter from Ted yesterday."

Archie's heart leapt. "Is he all right, my lady?"

"He sounds wonderfully well, Archie. They're putting on entertainments for the men, and he's been telling us what a good cheerful bunch they are. "

"Please my lady, they're lucky to. . ." he was interrupted by a loud urgent shout from somewhere near the kitchen garden.

"Help! Is anybody there? Help me!"

It was Dad's voice. Slithering on the ice, Archie ran. "Dad! I'm coming! Where are you?"

Dad was sprawled on a stretch of black ice, struggling to stand and falling again. The coachman, two footmen and two of Dad's assistants came to help. They made a stretcher out of an overcoat with poles in the sleeves and carried him to the Servants' Hall while Bertenshaw watched. Mr Grant telephoned the doctor, and by the time he got there quite a crowd had gathered at the back of the Hall. "This is going to make more work for the rest of us," muttered Bertenshaw to anyone who would listen. Inside, Archie stood at his father's side. So did Lady Hazelgrove.

"I'm afraid it's a break, and a bad one," said Dr Purdy. "We'll have to get you to hospital and have it put in plaster, then it'll be six weeks on crutches for you,

Sparrow. Six weeks at the least."

The car waited at the back door of the Hall to take Dad to hospital. Archie, who had never been in a car, was hoping he'd be able to go with him, but Dad told him to go on with his work.

"Tell Bertenshaw I want to see those paths gritted when I get back," growled Dad. "If there's ice the size of a pea I want it done again. It could have been Her Ladyship or anyone. Understood?"

The car growled away. Lady Hazelgrove turned to Archie.

"What did he mean about Bertenshaw?" she asked. "Was he supposed to have gritted the paths?"

Archie didn't like telling tales, but he was too angry with Bertenshaw to care. Anyway, Lady Hazelgrove had already guessed.

"Yes, my lady," he said.

"I see, Archie. Thank you." She walked away with a look of determination on her face.

"We'll make a bed downstairs for when your dad gets home," said Ma. "That's war for you. Gardeners going off to fight and we're left with the likes of Bertenshaw to keep things going. Did you know he got a final warning?"

"No, Ma!" A final warning was a serious thing. One more mistake from Bertenshaw and he'd be sacked. The cottage he lived in belonged to the Carrs, just as Gardener's Cottage did, so he'd be homeless too.

"My lady said if we weren't so short of staff she

48

would have dismissed him at once. All the staff are talking about it."

While Dad lay in the house and grumbled, Ma did what she could to help in the garden, pulling up weeds while Flora played with pebbles. Dad was soon on crutches, swinging his lame leg, then just on one crutch, always with a little frown of pain on his face, supervising work and giving orders. His leg was mending badly and taking a long time. Spring came slowly, but it came at last.

Never mind," he said one evening. "At least when I look like this, nobody's going to give me a white feather."

"Why a white feather?" asked Jenn.

"I'm surprised you haven't found out," said Ma. "I hear there's women in York handing them out."

"If a woman gives a man a white feather it's a way of saying he's a coward," said Dad. "If they see a man who's fighting age and not wearing a uniform, they give him a white feather to shame him."

"That's shocking!" said Jenn. "He could just be a bit poorly, or be a, like, a doctor or somebody that we need to be here, or anything. How do those women know?"

"Quite," said Ma. "There's enough bad things happening in the world now without stirring up more trouble. There'll be a lot more trouble before this year's out."

But for a while, the news after that was good. There were occasional letters from Master Ted, and soon all

49

the household was talking about them. He seemed to be well. A lot of the Ashlings men were under his command, and he was proud of them. Archie wanted to write to him and tell him what was happening at Ashlings, but he didn't know where to write. And there wasn't much to tell, except that the gardens were overrun with rabbits in spite of all that His Lordship's gun dogs, Brier and Sherlock, could do. Star didn't even try to chase them any more.

It was better when Star was being a nuisance, thought Archie as he watched him. He wished Star would be under everyone's feet again. There were nights when Archie lay awake wondering if Master Ted was being honest in his letters. He might be injured or hungry, and didn't want his family to know.

"I just met Her Ladyship in garden," said Dad one morning. "She was asking about new fruit trees int' walled garden. And she was telling me about Master Ted's letters, you'd think he was on holiday from what he says."

Soon afterwards Archie saw her, too, walking back towards the Hall with Connel unleashed but still walking at her side and Star behind her. Star didn't look himself, not at all. He walked slowly, with his head down. *Poor little soul*, thought Archie. *He must be missing Master Ted more than ever.* His walk slowed and slowed, and Archie stopped working to watch him. Then the dog's legs seemed to weaken. He stumbled, and rolled on to his side.

"My lady!" yelled Archie, and ran to Star. His nose was hot and dry, and his eyes were dull. Lady Hazelgrove was hurrying across the lawn to them.

"He just fell, my lady," said Archie. "He's not well."

Lady Hazelgrove knelt, felt Star's nose, and put a hand to his neck to find a pulse.

"He needs the vet," she said. "Archie, carry him back to the Hall for me. To the front door. Connel, come!"

Holding her long skirts in one hand she ran ahead of him to the Hall with Connel loping at her side. Archie gathered Star's limp, warm body in his arms and held him closely as he ran him to the Hall. Under his hand he could feel the fast beating of the small heart and suddenly it mattered, more than anything else in his life, more than anything in the world, that Star stayed alive.

"You'll be all right," he said. "You've got to be, haven't you? Your master's coming back for you. Hold on now, hold on for Master Ted." Then the chauffeur was running to the car and Lady Hazelgrove was taking the weak bundle of dog from Archie's arms.

He was working in the garden in the afternoon when Jenn came running to find him. She had just come in from school, she said, and "Lady Hazelgrove's at our cottage! She came to talk to Dad and she sounds dead cross!"

"Any news of Star?" he asked as they ran back to the cottage, but Jenn wasn't listening. The door of the front room was closed, and they heard the firm voice of Lady

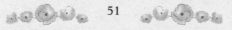

Hazelgrove. Archie and Jenn tiptoed up the stairs and sat on the middle stair to listen.

"What has happened to Star is bad enough!" exclaimed Lady Hazelgrove.

Something clenched in Archie's stomach. Star mustn't die. It was unthinkable. He had to be here for Master Ted coming home, he couldn't possibly die. He mattered too much, and not just for Master Ted's sake. Star was annoying, scruffy, and scatter-brained, but Archie, sitting on the stairs, knew that he was simply the nicest dog he had ever met.

"What's happened to Star?" whispered Jenn.

"Poorly," he whispered back.

"We could all have ended up eating poisoned rabbit," Lady Hazelgrove was saying. Archie felt suddenly sick with fear.

"My lady," said Dad, "let me assure you on my word, I have never used poisons on the gardens and I never will. I'm here to work with nature, not poison it. It's not my way. And the men have orders not to touch it either. You're welcome to inspect the sheds. All of them. You can search the house if you like, you'll find nothing. And the account books. I'll be doing a search myself, and pardon me saying so, my lady, but God help anyone who's put down poison on Ashlings land. Anywhere. You're quite right to say it's not just t'dogs." A harsher note entered his voice and Archie could hear that he was fighting down his anger. "Our little Flora's still tiny enough to put all sorts in her mouth."

Jenn pressed closer to Archie, who put his arm round her.

"Quite so," said Lady Hazelgrove more gently.

"We'll get straight on to it, my lady," he said. "I suggest a good place to start would be the chemists' shops round about. They have to keep a list of sales of poisons, and who they sell them to."

There was a rustle of skirts as Her Ladyship stood up. Archie and Jenn darted up the stairs and out of sight. When she had gone and Dad was alone, they crept back downstairs.

"Is Star all right?" asked Archie, and Dad didn't ask him if he'd been eavesdropping or tell him off.

"He might pull through, he might not," said Dad. "If I find out who put down poison on our land I won't be accountable for my actions."

Please let Star live. Please let him be all right. Archie repeated it over and over all day, and until he finally fell asleep that night. *He's a good dog, he'd never hurt anyone. If he were a lad he'd be a nice little lad.* The next day, the news was that Star was still alive, and there was hope. Lady Hazelgrove had stayed up all night with him. The day after that, Sam the Boots told Archie that Star was eating well and wagging his tail again, and Bertenshaw was sent for to come to the Hall.

"The chemist in Kirby Moss identified him," said Dad. "He used a false name, but the chemist gave a description. Turns out he's got quite a store of poisons. Says it's for rats. Little Star had a lucky escape."

"I don't like to see a man lose his job, but there's no excuse for that," said Ma firmly. "That dog nearly died and I don't like to think what else might have happened. Still, the old misery will have to work somewhere."

"He can always go to road mending," said Dad. "He's strong, he can work. And I reckon he'll move in with his old father. Lady Hazelgrove's given him two weeks to be out of the cottage, but he's not to show his face in the gardens meantime. We'll be even more short of staff now, but I still reckon we're better off without him."

It was as if Bertenshaw had been casting a shadow over the gardens, because everything seemed better after that. The weather was warming and the garden filled with colour. Lady Hazelgrove told them that she had to keep Master Ted's letters safe from Star or he'd take them to his bed. Then a telegram arrived.

Chapter Five

It was such a bright day, too, to begin with. The daffodils were sunshine-yellow trumpets against the green, and the garden was filled with every colour of spring. Dad could walk without crutches, though he still needed a stick and walked badly, and Archie enjoyed the way the whole family worked together in the garden to keep things looking as they should. Jenn would come in from school, change her pinafore, and get straight down to the greenhouses. Even Flora waddled about carrying empty plant pots.

Lady Hazelgrove was in the garden talking to Dad. She wanted to plant more fruit trees in the walled garden where they could sprawl against the warm brick walls in summer. Archie was supposed to be learning about pruning. Instead he was putting back the bulbs Star had dug up, but he was just glad that Star was still alive to be a nuisance. Star was now tucked under Lady Hazelgrove's arm so he couldn't do any more damage. They were interrupted by Mr Grant coming into the garden with some sort of paper in his hand.

"Telegram, my lady," he said, and Lady Hazelgrove handed Star to the person who was nearest, who was Archie.

Why did it suddenly feel as if a cloud had crossed the sun? Archie felt his father's hand on his shoulder, gently drawing him back, as if they should leave space round Her Ladyship.

Archie folded his lips tightly. Not all telegrams were bad news. It might mean that Master Ted was coming home. It might mean. . . He saw that Her Ladyship's hands were trembling.

"My lady?" said Grant. Archie held Star more tightly.

"My lady!" called Dad, as Lady Hazelgrove swayed and fell forward. Archie darted to help her, Dad hobbling behind him, and between them they caught her before she could land on the path. Dad was taking off his jacket and folding it to put under her head.

"Run to the Hall for help, Archie!" he ordered.

"Fetch Her Ladyship's maid!" called Mr Grant, kneeling stiffly beside Lady Hazelgrove. Archie put down Star and ran, Star running beside him because he thought something exciting was happening, and all the time in Archie's head was the picture of Lady Hazelgrove's white face and the telegram that had fallen from her hand. He had only glimpsed it for seconds, but he knew what it said.

REGRET TO INFORM YOU THAT YOUR SON CAPTAIN EDWARD CARR WAS KILLED IN ACTION ON 21 MARCH. HE WAS A FINE SOLDIER AND DIED NOBLY AND WITHOUT PAIN.

There was no Master Ted. There never would be again. It felt impossible, but it must be true.

March, just when the days were getting longer. March, with spring and summer coming and Master Ted would never see it. He'd never come home. He'd be buried, if he got a proper burial, in some muddy corner of France.

At Ashlings Hall it was as if everything in the world had turned to grey. Grey as lead. Grey as death. Only last summer Master Ted and Star had never been far away, two happy, confident characters enjoying the grounds of Ashlings together. The war had stolen one and left the other sad and puzzled. War was a bully.

Lord Hazelgrove came back on leave from his army camp looking suddenly old. At Gardener's Cottage at nights Archie cried in the big lonely bed that he used to share with Will. There was no shame in crying for Master Ted. Everyone cried. At the Hall, Star still looked hopefully from the window.

So much for a useless little wooden sword. So much for Master Ted's lucky charm. It hadn't done him any

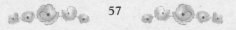

good. As a gardener's boy, Archie had learned to shoot the rabbits and crows that tried to eat the plants. He asked his dad if he could practise, and Dad set up tin cans for him to shoot at. *Bang.* I hate this war. *Bang.* Hate it. *Bang.* Day by day he got on with his work in the garden because he had to, but it was as if the sun would never come out again.

Every morning Archie woke up feeling that it couldn't be true. Master Ted couldn't die. He wasn't like ordinary men, he had twice as much life as anyone else. He was a hero, he was theirs. He belonged to Ashlings, not to the army, not to a bit of French mud. It couldn't be true. Somebody had made a mistake – but then a letter arrived from an officer. A shell had landed right on the trench where Master Ted and his men were based. Nobody survived. Frank Roger, the one all the girls fancied, had died with Master Ted.

"Please let him not be dead," said Archie in his prayers every night, because it was the only thing he could do for Master Ted now. If there'd been a funeral he and Dad could have sent flowers from the garden, Ma would have arranged them and they would have filled the little church with flowers, but they couldn't even do that for Master Ted, not even give him a funeral.

The day the bad news came for Lady Hazelgrove and Mrs Rogers, there were letters for the Ashlings estate, too. One was addressed to Mr and Mrs Sparrow at Gardener's Cottage, but the boy who was doing the post while the usual postman was away being a soldier didn't know his way around. Bertenshaw, sitting in the doorway of the cottage that he had to leave the next day, gruffly offered to help.

"Who's that for?" he asked. "Gardener Sparrow? Give it here. I'll give it him."

When the boy had gone away, Bertenshaw turned and trudged back to the cottage. Sparrow had got him sacked. Why should he do him any favours? He wasn't delivering letters to him.

He pushed the envelope into his pocket. It would get cool in the evening, and he had rubbish to burn. He'd have to light the stove.

Two weeks later was a sunny Sunday. Archie was thinking that it had no business to be so sunny when Master Ted was dead when Jenn came running in from Sunday school.

"Captain Bettany's here!" she said. "I saw the car, I saw him going to the house!"

"Maybe it's good news!" said Archie. "Maybe Master Ted's not. . ." but he stopped when he saw the way Jenn looked at him.

"He didn't look like good news," she said. "He looked miserable. And it was awful, because Star was at the window and he must have seen a soldier in uniform because he came running out. . ."

"Oh, bless him!" said Ma.

". . .then he jumped out at Captain Bettany, then he just sort of ran around him a bit and followed him into the house with his tail down."

59

At least we can understand that Master Ted's died, thought Archie. *Poor Star. He'll never understand it*. He spent the rest of the day hanging round the front door of the Hall as much as he could and dodging out of the way if Mr Grant was about. Ma had cooked one of their chickens for lunch and Archie took a few scraps from the larder to feed to Star when nobody was looking. Star liked it, and went on licking Archie's fingers after the chicken was finished. When Captain Bettany finally came out, looking tired and solemn, Archie ran to meet him.

"Sir?" he said. "Please, sir, you won't rem—"

"Yes I do," he said, and smiled, but his eyes remained sad. "You're the garden lad, aren't you?"

"Please," began Archie again, and didn't know how to go on.

Captain Bettany sat down on the doorstep. He patted the space beside him for Archie to sit down, too.

"I'll tell you what I just told Lord and Lady Hazelgrove," he said. "I was in the trench behind Ted's, I saw the shell land. By the time I got there the field ambulance had taken everyone off. I found his cap and what was left of his papers." He turned to look Archie in the eyes. "He was a good soldier. A good officer, his men would have done anything for him because he'd do anything for them."

He patted Archie's shoulder and went out to the car.

"Take care, sir!" said Archie and he realized how hard it must be for Captain Bettany to go back to those trenches, where the next shell might be for him.

Gardeners don't start wars. Neither did Master Ted, or Bettany, or Star for that matter, but they all got hurt. He rubbed the back of his hand across his eyes and turned for home, walking past the window where Star stood on a chair with his paws on the sill.

In the potting shed, Archie's eyes blurred. He rubbed and rubbed at the chalk lines on the wall until there was nothing but a grey mist.

Star was so used to the chair in the window that he thought of it now as his own. It was the place where he waited for Ted. Every night when Ted didn't come he went to guard his bedroom. His basket was still in there, with the door open, and he had furnished it from Master Ted's things. He had stolen a pillow that smelt of Ted, and always took Ted's towel and his boot to bed, too, and anything else he could find that was to do with his master. He loved that bed. It smelt right. And in the morning he would come back to his place at the window, so as not to miss Ted when he came home.

"It's not right." Dad was saying it as Archie went back into the house, grubby with chalk dust.

"What's not right?" asked Archie.

"Never you mind," snapped Ma. But the next morning, he found out.

Archie had never seen Star on a lead before. But in the morning, straightening up from digging, he saw Lady Hazelgrove walking through the rose garden to

Gardener's Cottage with Star walking on a lead, pulling away to sniff at the grass. Just Star, not Connel, and that was strange. Dad came to the door and took the lead and presently Lady Hazelgrove turned away and walked back to the Hall alone, drawing her black gloved hand across her eyes. Archie rammed his spade into the earth and ran to the cottage.

"Is Master Ted's dog coming to live with us?" he asked hopefully when he got into the kitchen. Star, lying on the hearthrug, beat his tail on the ground, and Archie knelt down to smooth his fur.

"Hello, Star," he said gently. "Have you come to see us?" Under his hands the dog felt thin.

"Don't pet him, Archie," said Ma, but she gave the dog a bit of biscuit. He licked it, but didn't eat.

"Archie, sit down," ordered Dad. He was sitting by the table with his bad leg stretched out in front of him. Archie sat down. At his feet, Star settled down with his head on his paws.

"As you're here, you'll have to be told," said Dad. "It's a hard thing for you to hear, but you're a big lad now. The whole world's in a right state, and there's things you have to understand. All these months that dog's been waiting for his master to come back, just as he did before Christmas. But this time Master Ted isn't coming back and the dog doesn't know that, he doesn't understand. He'll go on and on, sitting at that window all day, sleeping with Master Ted's things at night, and it's too hard on him. He's already losing his spirit. Look at him, he doesn't even eat as well as a dog should. The heart's going out of him. Lady Hazelgrove can't bear to watch him sitting at that window for one more day. She even said it would have been better if Bertenshaw's poison had finished him off. She wants it to be over, so she brought him to me. Do you understand? It has to be over."

Archie looked past his father. The gun lay propped against the door.

"No," he said.

"It has to be done," said Dad. "Mind, Jenn and Flora mustn't know a word of this."

Ma put a hand on Archie's shoulder.

"I know it's hard," she said, "but it's for the best. And it's not up to us. Now that Master Ted's gone he's Her Ladyship's dog, and she's given her orders. It's hard enough for them to handle their own mourning without the dog grieving for his master too."

Dad got up stiffly, limped to the back door and opened it.

"Star, heel," he commanded. The dog stood up and walked slowly, his ears and tail down.

"No!" Archie swooped down on Star, wrapping him in his arms and bending his head over the soft, curled coat. "Star, you stay with me! You can't, Dad!"

Star looked up and from side to side. He tried to wriggle free, but Archie held on, hugging him firmly.

"Archie, let him go," said Ma. "Don't make this worse."

"He won't know a thing about it," Dad told him. He picked up the gun. "One second he's here, the next he's

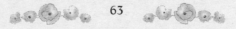

dead. He won't suffer. One shot to the head, and it's all done with."

"He'll be off to heaven to find his master," said Ma, but Archie pressed his cheek against Star's warm head. Master Ted shouldn't be in heaven, not yet. He should be playing cricket somewhere with Star running to field the ball.

"And what would Master Ted say?" he demanded. "What would he say, if he knew you'd killed his dog?"

"Archie, be a man," said Ma.

Tearfully he turned to face her. He still held on to Star.

"I am being a man! I'm protecting Master Ted's dog, and I'm not going to let anyone hurt him! I'm not letting go!"

"Now, Archie, this isn't fair," said Ma quietly. "This is hard enough for your dad already." Dad waited at the back door with the gun in his hand.

"Dad doesn't have to do it," insisted Archie. "I know he's missing his master, but Star's a good dog, he's a healthy dog. He just needs someone to be his friend, like Master Ted was. He needs time. Please? Can't we keep him?"

"When Her Ladyship's given orders to put him down?" said Ma. "If your dad doesn't do it, she'll only ask somebody else."

"No!" cried Archie fiercely and curled himself round the dog. He reached into his pocket. There was an empty toffee bag in there, a bit sticky and fluffy, but it would still taste of toffee. He held it in front of Star, who licked it, and kept licking, then turned his tongue to Archie's sticky fingers.

"Oh, our Archie!" said Ma in disgust, but Dad only watched.

"I said myself it wasn't right to shoot him," he said at last.

"Her Ladyship's a sensible woman and she said it was cruel to let him live," said Ma. "Poor little thing, expecting his master to come back. He's a dog, he doesn't understand."

"Maybe," admitted Dad. "But if he could get attached to Master Ted he could maybe get attached to our Archie, given a chance."

"He's already attached to me," said Archie. "I've given him bits of food. I've thrown things for him to fetch and everything."

"Her Ladyship. . ." began Ma.

"Her Ladyship doesn't need to know," said Dad firmly. He took a step towards Archie, who hugged the dog more closely. "Now, son, listen to me. I'm going to lock this gun away in the cupboard. When I get back, I don't want to know where that dog is. Nobody's to know about him. If any of the staff see him, we're in trouble."

"An invisible dog," said Ma with a sigh, when Dad had gone. "That's what he'll have to be. Your invisible dog." She shook her head. "Ridiculous. I daresay most of the ground staff would pretend they hadn't seen him, but you can't take chances. Your father reckons a dog's more trouble than it's worth in a garden, digging things up and doing its business where it shouldn't. I don't see how you're going to exercise it without folks knowing. What will you do if it barks?" But then she almost smiled. "I like a dog about the place but they're supposed to live outside in a kennel, and that thing's used to being in a house. You'll have your hands full with it. I've never even seen it walk to heel for more than two seconds, it might be unteachable by now. Heaven help it, it's as daft as a brush."

Archie had never trained a dog by himself, but years before he had watched Lord Hazelgrove working with Brier and Sherlock. He'd manage somehow. Dad had said he didn't want to know where Star was, so Archie was about to carry the dog up to his room. Then he thought again, stood up, and patted his leg.

"Come on, Star," he said. "Heel!"

Star sat still.

"Walk away from him, Archie," said Ma.

Archie left the room. Nothing happened. He walked back in to see Star sitting with his head on one side as if puzzled. He wouldn't whistle, not after what had happened last time.

"Star!" he called brightly. "Heel! Come on!"

Star still sat. He knew exactly what he was being asked to do. He just couldn't understand why. This wasn't his house, or his boy.

"Look at it," said Ma. "It must have been dropped on its head when it were a pup. Take a bit of stick from the firewood, Archie, see if he wants to play with it."

Archie took a chunky piece of wood and waved it. This time Star lolloped upstairs after him and lay on the

bedroom floor, chewing the wood.

"I'll have to find you somewhere to sleep," said Archie. "You'll need a bed up here where nobody can see it." He sat on his bed and watched Star gnawing contentedly at the lump of wood, holding it still with one paw.

"I've got a dog," Archie said. For the first time since the telegram he felt a warm smile begin inside him and spread to his face. "I've got a dog. And it's you, you daft article. But you're Master Ted's daft article." And he made a promise, raising his head and his voice. "Wherever you are, Master Ted, don't you worry about your dog. I'll look after him."

Master Ted? Star left his new toy and trotted to the window, and put his paws on the sill so that Archie felt painfully sorry for him. He'd have to look out for that – take care how he mentioned Master Ted's name in front of Star.

"I miss him too," he said. "We'll look after each other. You're a good dog."

He made Star a bed with a bit of old blanket in a corner of the bedroom floor, but Star didn't seem to know what it was for. He was more interested in Archie. Without Ted or Her Ladyship, Archie seemed to be the person to stay close to. But Dad had said that he didn't want to see Star when he came back, so the dog would have to stay upstairs while Archie went back to work. He sat Star firmly on the blanket.

"Star, stay!" he commanded, holding out his hand,

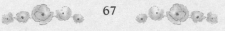

palm forwards. He walked away.

"Good dog," he said, then realized that, to Star, "good dog" meant that he'd done what he was asked to do and could stop doing it now. Star was up and trotting to his side. Archie picked him up and sat him on the blanket again.

"You're supposed to stay stayed," he said. "Stay!"

Star began to follow him. He turned.

"Stay!" he said as firmly as he could. "Stay!"

This time Star stayed put, but Archie hated leaving him. It seemed cruel. But Star would have to get used to staying up there alone.

"Ma," he asked when he was back in the kitchen, "will it cost a lot of money to feed him?"

Ma smiled. "I daresay we can afford him if he's not too fussy," she said.

"Only, I want to pay," he said. "I've got pocket money. I want to be a proper owner."

She shrugged. "It won't come to much," she said. "Neither here nor there."

"But I want to," insisted Archie.

"You're as daft as he is," she said. "We'll see what he costs to feed, but it'll be no more than pennies. How are you going to walk him without anyone seeing?"

"Take him early in the morning and late at night, after dark," he suggested.

"After dark? That thing could get lost in broad daylight. And gamekeeper would have something to say if he reckoned somebody was tramping about at night."

"Then I'll take him right away behind the gardens,

through the spinney and over the road into Little Keld Wood," he said. "I'd take him there wrapped in my coat so nobody could see him. Or I could. . ." he stopped and listened. "Is that Flora?"

Somewhere upstairs, somebody was moaning. That wasn't Flora! There was a whimper, and Archie took the stairs two at a time with Ma following.

Star had had enough of sitting and staying. He'd waited for a long time, lonely, confused and in a strange place. He was unhappy, and saying so.

"Come here, Star," said Archie. Star ran to him at once, tail wagging, putting his paws up on Archie's knees.

"Good boy," said Archie. "Good dog."

Star turned his head and licked Archie's wrist, and in that moment everything about Star made sense to Archie. He saw him the way Master Ted had seen him. It didn't matter that Star was little and daft, and as mongrel as any village lad's dog. He was just a small dog who needed a good friend to look after him.

"You're a grand dog, you," he said. "You're the best."

Ma shook her head. "We'll have to swear our Jenn to secrecy," she said. "I don't know what we'll do about Flora. Just yet there's only us can understand a word she says, but one of those words is 'dog'."

Later that day Archie put on an old jacket of Dad's and stuffed a handful of broken biscuit into the pocket. The jacket was threadbare and too big for him, but there was room to smuggle Star underneath it. They were across the road and deep into Little Keld Wood before he put the dog down.

It was a long time since Archie had been in this wood, and the scent of damp grass and growing trees woke up his love for it. There had been a time when he and Will were forbidden to play here because they always came home with torn trousers from climbing trees and mud on the seats of their trousers from sliding down the bank. Wet feet, too, if they couldn't stop at the bottom. They were magic, these woods, like the woods in a story. He knew where the badger sett was, and where the heron fished. In May the air would be heady with bluebells, and the wide overgrowing rhododendrons made caves were he and Will used to hide or chase each other.

"And it's somewhere you probably never went with you-know-who," said Archie. "So maybe you won't be looking for him here. You have a good run."

Star began to sniff and search. There were trails to follow. He liked this new and fascinating place, and his curiosity woke up for the first time since Master Ted had gone away. He sniffed. There were leaves and grass and a scent of badger and fox – and there was a stick, just the kind that he liked! With difficulty, because it was big and awkward to carry, he took it to Archie to throw.

With every throw of the stick, Star enjoyed this game more. Each time Archie threw harder and further and each time Star brought it back like a trophy, dropped it at his feet, and watched with bright eyes for the next throw. Because Star was happy, so was Archie.

"We're a great team, aren't we Star?" said Archie, picking up the stick for what might have been the tenth time. He realized that he'd stopped thinking about Master Ted. "You ready?"

When the game had been going on for about half an hour and Star had had enough time to run off some energy, Archie took the stick from him and held it behind his back. Star seemed to know what was expected, so he sat down.

"Sit!" ordered Archie. Star was doing it anyway, but it would help him to connect the word with the action. After they'd practised this a few times, Archie tried "sit and stay", walking a little further away from Star all the time. Half the time Star was only interested in finding more sticks, but after a lot of patience and broken biscuits he would stay, sitting up and alert and waiting for Archie to call him. Archie whistled, too, but this time it wasn't Master Ted's whistle. He'd seen what that did to Star before, and couldn't bear it to happen again so instead he whistled one long note and one short one, knowing that to begin with it wouldn't mean anything to Star – but in time it would. They were in this for life, after all.

"It's been long enough now, Star," said Archie at last. "Come on, then. Heel! Are you bringing your stick home?"

He bundled Star under the jacket before they crossed the road. They were nearly at Gardener's Cottage when he heard the trundling of a wheelbarrow and slipped behind a potting shed. One of the gardeners was on his way past with a barrow full of potted plants. Archie waited until he was out of the way before running down the path, past Ma's poultry shed, across the yard and in at the back door. A wheelbarrow would be a good way of moving Star about in future, if the dog would only stay in it.

"Dry its paws," said Ma quietly when they got back. "Look at you, Archie, you've got mud all down your front."

Star stood patiently to be towelled, then trotted to the front door and sat down as if it was time to go home to the Hall. When nobody opened it and Archie put a bowl of water on the floor he remembered that he was thirsty, and would be glad of a drink. A very pleasant smell was filtering into the air, too, a smell of meat cooking.

A small creature was on the floor, somebody not much bigger than he was. Star, already confused, sniffed at it, and drew back nervously when it reached out to touch him. It smelt human, but there was a sort of milky puppy scent about it too. He retreated away from it and watched Archie. Nothing about this place was familiar to him, but he felt safe with Archie and watched him all the time, getting up to follow him if he was out of sight. When Archie went outside to the privy, Star whined at the door. Jenn laughed.

"That dog loves our Archie," she said.

"There's no dog here," said Ma firmly, and put a few spoonsful of mince and potatoes to one side to cool down. Archie had barely opened the door to come back in again when Star leapt at him for joy, his paws on Archie's knees and his tail wagging furiously. Archie was back!

"My word," said Ma. "I never thought I'd see that. Reckon he's just relieved to see somebody he knows. Wash your hands, the pair of you, tea's nearly ready. Archie, that mince in the bowl, that's for somebody who isn't here."

Star sniffed uncertainly at the food. He liked Archie even more for feeding him, but couldn't quite understand why he was eating here, and not at the Hall. He sat back warily. The food was hot and didn't have the familiar smell of the Hall kitchens, but when he had tasted it the instinct to eat overcame him so that by the time Archie took the bowl away he had licked it clean and then licked it all round again, just for the taste. Then he sat at the front door wagging his tail. He had had a very exciting day out, and was ready for Her Ladyship to take him home. But she didn't come. Well, Archie would do for now. He felt safe with Archie.

After dark Archie checked to make sure that nobody was about then clipped on Star's lead and took him for a last walk before bedtime. Star pulled eagerly towards the Hall and barked.

"Shh!" Archie put his hand in front of the dog's face and glanced round to see if anyone had heard. Star stopped barking but he was annoyed and tried to dodge round the hand, determined to find his way home.

"Daft lummox," muttered Archie, and picked him up. In future he'd just have to take Star round the back of the cottage for a wee last thing at night. Soon it would be time to go to bed, and tonight Archie was looking forward to bedtime. Star would be sleeping in his room beside him. But as soon as they were back indoors Star pressed against the door and whimpered to be out again.

"Oh, bless him!" cried Ma. "He thinks he still lives at the Hall. Reckon we can't expect him to learn fast." She offered him some stale bread, but Star didn't want bread. He wanted to go home to Ted's room. When Archie called him upstairs he refused to step away from the door, not for food, not even for a stick.

"Can't sit there all night," said Archie at last. He gathered up Star in his arms, carried him upstairs and put him down on the blanket, but Star ran straight to the bedroom door and whimpered to be out.

Archie had had a long day, and had been outside for most of it. In spite of Star's fretting he was drifting off to sleep when he heard the pattering of paws, then a scrape and scuffle. Star was pushing and pulling the blanket to make it comfortable. He fell asleep to the sound of Star's quiet breathing and the odd little snuffle in his sleep and woke next morning to Star climbing on his bed and licking his face.

"You're more trouble than you're worth, you," said Archie sleepily, but he was smiling. He draped an arm over the dog and drifted back to sleep until Star scrabbled at the door to be out.

Star had woken him up so early that by the time Archie took the vegetables to the Hall it felt like lunchtime. At the back door he met Aggie the kitchenmaid on her way out, carrying a dog basket.

"What's that for?" he asked.

Aggie rubbed the back of her hand across her red-rimmed eyes.

"It's little Star's bed," she said. "Poor little mite. Her Ladyship says she can't bear to see this bed again and it's to go straight in the rubbish heap. He even had one of Master Ted's boots in there, so she kept that. I don't know how your father could bear to do it."

Archie took the basket from her. "I'll put it in the rubbish for you, Aggie," he said.

At the sight of his own basket Star felt at home for the first time since he came to Gardener's Cottage. He scrambled up the stairs after Archie, reaching up for the basket with both paws because Archie couldn't put it down fast enough for him.

He had a good scrape about. Ted's boot was gone but he still had the pillow, a sock that he'd hidden in there, and the towel. With Archie, his basket and his tokens of Ted, Star felt he could manage for now. Just until Ted came back.

Chapter Six

The next evening Archie poured a little lamp oil into a saucer and added some soot scraped from the fireplace. Star was used to being groomed and fussed, and didn't mind having his ears and paws rubbed as Archie worked the paste into his fur. At last Archie sat back to review his work, but he was disappointed. The idea of all this messy, sooty stuff had been to disguise Star in case anyone saw him, but now he just looked like the same dog with a few dark grey patches. There was no disguising Star's face, his expression, his way of watching you and wagging his tail because he was expecting something good to happen. If he opened his mouth it would be Star's bark, too, and at the end of it all Archie was sootier than the dog. Ma folded her arms and looked at Star with her head on one side.

"That Star," she said, "that dog of Master Ted's that your father put to sleep, he was one of a whole litter. Four or five of them, I heard, all mongrel pups. I don't know where the others went, but I reckon they would all look much the same."

For a moment Archie didn't know why she was saying this, but then he understood. "That's right," he said. "This one looks like Master Ted's dog 'cause it's his brother from the same litter. This one's got more markings on it." He worked more soot into the mark on Star's head. "And he's called. . ."

He couldn't shout "Star" anywhere on the Ashlings estate, but he'd need a name that sounded like "Star" so that the dog would still recognize it. He began to work his way through the alphabet, and didn't have to go far.

"Carr. If anyone asks he's called Carr, after the family."

"But you'll still have to keep him secret, son," said Ma. "Not everybody would fall for it. They'd be more likely to wonder why you've suddenly got a dog when the family have just lost one. You only tell that story if you have to. And you'll have to teach it to keep quiet."

Archie didn't mind telling a lie to protect Star, but Ma helping him in it didn't seem right. Mothers weren't supposed to help you lie. But then Ma went back to pretending the dog didn't exist, and Archie and Star grew into a pattern. It was easy to exercise Star in Little Keld Wood, far from the Hall. The only problem was getting him there, but he didn't mind being tucked under Archie's coat or wheeled in a barrow and covered with a bit of tarpaulin.

Within a week of Star coming to Archie, the new whistle was taking effect. Archie would watch the dog race off through the woods for the pure fun of running and veer round at the sound of the one-long-one-short whistle. Getting Star to come to heel was easy, but getting him to stay there for more than a few paces was all but impossible. He had made a lead out of a bit of rope, but Star didn't appear to understand leads, or the idea that he was meant to walk forward on them.

"You have to learn it," said Archie one afternoon. "I can't let you go running about off the lead anywhere else but here, ever. You have to get used to it. Star – I mean, Carr – Heel!"

He began to walk, and Star followed obediently at his heel until he caught sight of a butterfly on Archie's right and lurched at it. Archie tripped over the lead and fell sprawling in the moss. A second time he saw a rabbit and tugged so suddenly on the lead that the rope sheared painfully across Archie's palm, and a third time he tried to dodge behind Archie to pick up a stone. Finally, Archie sat down.

"What am I going to do with you?" he said, not for the first time. "You're more trouble than you're worth." Every day he said these words to Star, and every day he knew that he didn't mean them. Sitting with moss stains on his clothes and a graze on his hand, he ruffled Star's ears. Star could never be more trouble than he was worth. He was worth everything, even if he never did learn to walk to heel.

"What did I ever do before?" said Archie as Star rolled over to have his tummy tickled. "What did I do before I had you?"

Star learned to be quiet when Archie held up his hand. He would sit watching Archie, enjoying this new game of being silent, waiting for a bit of biscuit as a reward. But why did he have to be silent when Archie came back from work? Star would sense the time. He couldn't understand why Ma shut doors so that he couldn't look out of a window but he knew when Archie was due home and sat hopefully, listening for his step, his tail wagging hard.

Archie had never loved homecomings so much. Before the kitchen door shut behind him Star would be in his arms, licking and wriggling as if Archie was all any dog could want in the world. Nothing had ever made Archie feel as good as this, nothing. Star was discovering life again, splashing about in the joy of being a dog, and the splashes reached Archie.

"You're a good dog," he would say as Star jumped down from his arms, turned round, and put his paws up to Archie's knees. "Best dog in the world, you."

It took weeks, but Star began to find that life waiting for Ted was not only possible, but even happy sometimes. Archie was learning that, too. In Little Keld Wood Star discovered the places Archie had always loved. There was always something new, a scent to follow or a bird to chase, and Archie was always there with him to whistle and throw sticks, and run through the trees beside him. He loved it. His energy returned, and so did his appetite. He splashed in the beck and scampered over the forest floor. He learned to love the fireside at Gardener's Cottage, where he would dry off after a splash in the beck. Archie would carefully sweep up white hairs from the hearthrug and add a little more sooty paste to Star's thick coat.

Often, by the time they came back from the wood, Star would be trailing sticky goose-grass and have burrs in his ears. The first time this happened Archie found an old hairbrush with a broken handle and tried to groom him, but as Star wouldn't keep still and tried to eat the brush it wasn't a great success. Star seemed to groom himself, though. Somehow he always ended up clean.

By the end of the first week, Star had stopped crying for the Hall. If anyone came to the door, somebody – usually Ma – would hide him upstairs before opening it and now that his basket was in there, he quite liked Archie's room. He started taking Archie's socks to bed, too. Jenn, who had finished a scarf for a soldier and was learning to knit socks, made him a woollen pom-pom which he carried around even though it made him sneeze. But Archie was the one who fed and walked him.

Sometimes when a walk was over and he was wheeling a barrow home with Star hidden under a tarpaulin, Archie felt guilty. He was happy, and he shouldn't be, not when Master Ted was dead. He could still feel the raw place in his heart where Master Ted had been torn away, and yet he could be happy, too, with Star. It was puzzling, but that's the way it was.

Dad's leg still troubled him. Ma said that it hadn't set properly and he should see the doctor again, but Dad wouldn't have it. On his worst days, he stayed indoors drawing plans for the new sunken garden.

"We're going to build it for Master Ted," he said. "The Edward Carr Memorial Garden. I talked to Her Ladyship about it and she likes the idea. And she said Miss Julia – I should say, Lady Dunkeld – is coming here next week, so she'll have something to say about it. She has something to say about most things."

"She might bring our Will with her!" exclaimed Ma, then added quickly. "What am I saying? Of course she won't."

Of course Lady Dunkeld wouldn't bring the garden boy with her. But Archie longed to see Will again and knew how much Ma did, too.

Lady Dunkeld arrived the next Monday with Dunn, her chauffeur, a small grey-haired man who rarely spoke. On Tuesday Sam the Boots ran through the gardens shouting.

"Archie, where's your dad?" he yelled.

"Kitchen garden!" Archie shouted back.

"I'll get him, you fetch your ma!" called Sam. "They have to go the Hall, now!"

When Ma and Dad came back from the Hall, Ma was grey-white in the face. She held Flora balanced

on one hip and held tightly to Dad's hand on the other side. Dad looked worse than worried. He looked afraid, and Dad was never afraid. Even little Flora was solemn-faced, as if she knew something was wrong. Archie ran to take Flora because Ma looked as if she might drop her. Had someone else died?

"Open the door for your ma," said Dad. Archie ran upstairs to let Star out of the bedroom before he could start barking, and when he came down Dad was settling Ma into a chair.

"Put kettle on," ordered Dad. "It's our Will. Now, let's not panic. He's all right as far as we know. He's off somewhere. Her Ladyship asked Lady Dunkeld how our Will's doing, and Lady Dunkeld was surprised she asked. She thought Will was back here. He'd told her he wanted to come back and help me now that my leg was bad, and he was homesick and all. She gave him his train fare home."

"But he didn't come here," said Ma, and pressed the heel of her hand against one eye, then the other. "You know what he's done, don't you? He's found the nearest army camp and gone to be a soldier. No doubt he said he were old enough and they believed him."

"Lady Hazelgrove's sorting it out," said Dad. "She's got straight on the phone to His Lordship and Master Simon, and they'll soon get it sorted."

"But he'll be in France!" cried Ma.

"No he won't," said Dad. "He'll be in a training camp learning to do his shooting and marching. He won't be anywhere near a troop ship yet."

Ma sniffed. "He could have told us," she said. "He could have written us a letter."

"Aye, he could and he should," said Dad, "and when we get him home you can give him merry hell. And we will get him home. Lady Hazelgrove will sort it."

But the next day there was no word of Will. Lady Hazelgrove spent the morning making telephone calls, so that Ma and Dad were embarrassed about how much trouble she was taking. Nobody knew anything about a recruit called William Sparrow.

"He must have taken a different name," said Dad. He drummed his fingers on the kitchen table and looked out at the rain pelting down the window. "I'll go. I'm no use here, not with this leg. He's my boy, my problem, not Her Ladyship's. I'll have a word with her in the morning."

Archie knew that, and knew what to do next. He didn't know how to go about it, though, so he waited until Flora was asleep and Ma was tucking Jenn into bed. Only he and Dad were left downstairs.

"Dad," he said, "the estate can't spare you and neither can Ma. I'll go and find Will for you."

Dad stared at him so fiercely that Archie wanted to take a step back. Then Dad's face softened, and he laughed.

"Cheeky little beggar," he said. "You always wanted to do what you saw me doing. You were hardly walking when you wanted to dig with a full-sized spade. Never mind, son. I won't send a boy to do a man's job."

"The garden's a man's job," said Archie. "There's not

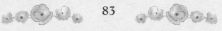

many of us any more, and it's the growing season. It'll be rubbish, Dad, without you. You give the orders, you see what wants doing. I can't do that, but I can find our Will."

"WHAT?"

The word fired into the back of Archie's head like gunshot. Ma was behind him with her hands on her hips and fire in her eyes.

"Isn't it bad enough?" she demanded. "I've got one son running away to be shot at, and you have to take yourself off as well?"

"I don't want to be a soldier, Ma!" he insisted. "I only want to find Will and stop him!"

"That's your father's job," she began, but she stopped suddenly and Archie could see that she was thinking exactly what he thought himself. Dad couldn't go looking for Will.

"I'll go," she said. "I'll go looking for Will and heaven help him when I find him."

"You can't," said Archie. "What about Flora?"

"Jenn can look after her."

"Jenn can't do everything. She can't do all the cooking."

"She'll have to learn. Archie, that dog – I mean, that dog that isn't there, that we don't know about – is sitting at back door with its paws crossed. Go and let him out."

There was no point in arguing with Ma. He still tried, right up until he went to bed, but her mind was made up. There was only one thing to do.

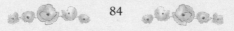

84

After an early morning walk with Star, Archie scrubbed himself clean and went to the Hall. He was lucky to meet Mr Grant the butler at the back door.

"Please, Mr Grant," he asked, "may I see Lady Hazelgrove? Or Lady Dunkeld?"

He was relieved to find that it would be Lady Hazelgrove, as he was a bit scared of Lady Dunkeld, who could be bossy. He was sent to the morning room and stood very awkwardly, his feet neatly together, hoping that he'd got his boots clean enough to leave no mud on the carpet. It was such a thick carpet, too, like walking on turf. Connel lay there in the sunshine.

Lady Hazelgrove's eyes looked small and pink. He guessed that she had been crying for Master Ted, and it made him embarrassed to look at her.

"Please, my lady," he said. "It's about our Will. I need to find him before he can go off to France."

"Lord Hazelgrove and I will find him," she said. "Recruits have to do three months training before they go to France, and we will have tracked him by then."

"But if he's using a false name he could be anywhere," he said. "Somebody who knows him has to go and look for him, somebody who'll recognize him, my lady. Dad can't go, you need him here, and Ma can't leave the girls."

"Indeed," she said. Connel raised her head and sniffed the air.

"Please, my lady," he said, "I reckon our Will would have gone to a camp near where Lady Dunkeld lives. I reckon he's still down south."

She almost smiled. "'Down south' is a big place, Archie."

Connel scrambled to her paws, wagging her tail. She raised her shaggy head, looking from one side to the other.

"Poor Connel," said Lady Hazelgrove. "She misses Star. She's looking for him."

Archie felt his face glow with heat and hoped it didn't show. Silently he willed Connel to leave him alone, but she was padding to his side, twitching her nose and wagging her tail.

"Connel likes you," observed Lady Hazelgrove. Connel hunted all round Archie, pushing her nose hard against his jacket. "She doesn't usually do that."

"She knows I like her, my lady," muttered Archie as Connel sat down on his foot and pressed her face against his side.

"So, Archie, how do you presume to get to Kent?"

Archie was too embarrassed to answer and he was distracted by Connel. She clearly knew all about Star, and had such an intelligent look about her that she might have started talking. Finally he managed to whisper, "I don't know, my lady."

"Did you want permission to travel with Lady Dunkeld?"

He'd thought about exactly that, but he hadn't dared ask. Fortunately she spared him from having to answer.

"I will have a word with Julia," she said. "Maybe you can go with her. But you should know. . ."

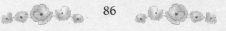

The door swung open. Lady Dunkeld strode in like a headmaster.

"Morning, Mother," she said breezily. "I'm all ready to go."

"Julia, do you remember Archie?" said Lady Hazelgrove. "Will Sparrow's brother? He wants to come with you and go looking for Will."

Lady Dunkeld stood back and looked Archie up and down.

"Jolly good idea," she announced. "And when you find him give him a walloping from me. I'll scoop him up, shall I, Mother, and take him with me?" Without waiting for an answer, she went on, "but I have to tell you, Archie, I'm turning Fivewells – that's our Kent house – into a nursing home for wounded soldiers. The place is already full of officers and nurses. I can't squash another body in anywhere, so goodness knows where we'll put you."

"I'll sleep in a shed or anything, my lady!" said Archie.

"You'll have to. And if you're going to go hunting for your brother you'll have to do it by yourself because we can't spare anyone to help you."

"Julia!" said Lady Hazlegrove. "He's only a boy!"

"Boys grow up quickly in wartime," said Lady Dunkeld. "Archie, can you ride a bicycle?"

He hesitated, gently pushing Connel's nose away. Master Ted had sort of taught him how to ride a bicycle, but there had been a lot of falling off.

"If you can't, you'll have to learn," she said briskly.

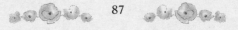

"Either that, or walk everywhere. When you're not cycling all over the place to find your brother, you can do a bit of gardening to earn your keep. Do the work Will would have been doing if he hadn't taken the king's shilling. Off you go, then, you've got half an hour to pack. I'll tell my chauffeur to bring the car round."

"Thank you, my lady – my ladies!"

In the potting shed at Fivewells the windows rattled and there was a smell of earth and damp plant pots. Archie's bed was a soldier's camp bed with a pillow and a few blankets, and when he finally flopped into it, it felt like heaven. Anywhere would have done, anywhere he could just lie down and shut his eyes. Star settled down beside him with a sigh.

Leaving home had been dramatic. Ma had flown into such a rage that Flora had burst into tears and Jenn had had to grab her and run outside. Dad had come in to see what the fuss was about and quietly pointed out that Archie wasn't leaving for ever, he was only going to find Will. Then Ma had stopped raging at Archie and grumbled at Dad instead until Archie said he had to be out in less than half an hour, and could he have a sandwich to take with him, please? Ma started to say that he could get his own sandwich, but then she suddenly stopped scolding and started mothering. She filled a basket with so much bread, ham, cheese and fruit that he felt he'd be embarrassed to take it with him, but it would be enough for two. When he picked up Star's bowl she looked up from cramming pie into the basket.

"You can't take him with you!"

"He'll have to," said Dad. "There's nobody here to go smuggling him to the woods three times a day."

Archie hadn't been thinking about whether to take Star. They'd both lost Master Ted, and didn't want to lose each other. Of course they couldn't be separated. Where Archie went, Star went. He'd already worked out what to do.

There had been hugs, with Ma trying not to cry and Dad telling him to find that young monkey sharpish and get home. Ma had said that if she had Will in front of her she'd knock him into the middle of next week, but Archie knew that really if she had Will in front of her she'd hug the breath out of him. Dad had slipped him some pocket money and told him not to keep Lady Dunkeld waiting. Lady Hazelgrove had had the idea of writing a letter about Will and asking Dad to write one too, to prove that Will was underage for the army.

"How long do you think you're coming for?" demanded Lady Dunkeld when Archie arrived. He was carrying a carpet bag, a covered basket, and a straw shopping bag which he held bundled in the crook of his arm. "Throw your stuff in the back and hop in. You're in the back, I like to sit up front beside Dunn when I'm not driving myself. Dunn's my chauffeur, by the way, but don't distract him when he's driving."

Archie did as he was told, his heart quickening with excitement. His first-ever ride in a motor car. He placed the bag on the seat beside him.

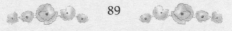

By the time they were a few miles clear of the village he had been wishing he'd never seen the car. He'd closed his eyes and taken deep breaths because that was what Ma always told him to do when he felt ill. With his eyes shut he couldn't see the countryside hurtling by so fast, which helped, but he could still feel every lurch and jolt on the road and the relentless churning of the engine. He had forced himself not to think about being sick. He had nothing to be sick into, and as for the inside of the car with the shiny leather seats . . . he'd never be forgiven if he threw up in there.

He had kept the basket with Star in close by his side. He hadn't asked Lady Dunkeld if he could bring his dog, not so much in case she guessed that it was Star, but because she might say no. At last, just when he felt he had been in the growling belly of a beast for years and it would never end, the car had slowed and jerked to a stop. Archie had opened his eyes, hoping that this was Kent.

"Good heavens, you look rough!" exclaimed Lady Dunkeld. "Never been in a car before?"

"No, my lady."

"Poor old Archie! Never mind. You'll get used to it."

The house where they had stopped didn't look like a family home. They were in a small town, outside a hotel with "The Royal George" on a sign at the door.

"Where are we, my lady?" he had asked.

"Market Willoughby," she replied promptly. "Good place to stop for lunch. You and Dunn can eat in the staffroom."

"I don't want anything, thank you, my lady." He didn't even want to think about food.

She looked sternly at him. "I can't have you wasting away," she said. "Dunn, will you make sure. . . Good heavens! What's that?"

The straw shopping bag was moving. Star, wrapped in a towel inside it, had slept all the way. Now that the car had stopped, he needed to know what was happening. Wearing the bag like a hood he licked Archie's wrist, and wagged his tail. He had just decided that Archie was there, so everything must be all right, when he recognized somebody else he knew, and launched himself so eagerly at Lady Dunkeld that she had to take a step back to steady herself. She caught him and fussed him, but she was looking at Archie.

"Archie Sparrow!" she cried in a voice so loud that women on the other side of the road turned to look. "Get out of the car and come here!"

Archie did as he was told. Star was tucked firmly under Lady Dunkeld's arm.

"Archie," she said firmly. "This looks very like my brother's dog."

Archie had his lie ready, but he still stammered as he gave it out. "No, my lady, he's from the same litter. My Dad got him. He's very like Master Ted's dog, my lady. Lady Hazelgrove had that other dog shot, my lady."

Her face was still stern. "What do you call him?"

"We called him 'Carr' after the family, my lady."

"Let's see," she said, and put Star down. "Carr! Sit!" Star who was used to having two names by now,

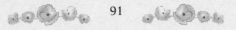

knew what to do. He sat down with his head on one side, wondering what was coming next.

"Good lad, Carr," said Archie.

There was a snort of laughter from Dunn. "Good name for it, my lady," he said. "Looks like it should be on wheels."

Lady Dunkeld gave an unladylike guffaw of a laugh. "He's your problem, not mine, Archie," she said. "Make sure he behaves himself."

She marched into the hotel for lunch. The chauffeur went in through a different door and later brought Archie a pie, which he fed to Star. There was a water fountain in the town square, and after a walk to that and a drink for Star and himself, Archie had felt a bit better.

"Sit up at the front with us," Lady Dunkeld had said when they were ready to go. "You'll feel better up here."

"Bit crowded, my lady," remarked Dunn.

"Be quiet and drive the car," she had said. So Archie had sat beside her feeling the wind in his hair as the car roared on. This was like flying, Star was on his lap, and Archie had wanted it to last for ever. When they stopped again his stomach was growling with hunger, but while Lady Dunkeld and Dunn found somewhere to eat he stayed put and shared his food from home with Star. By the time they reached Fivewells he had drifted into a sleep in which he felt cold except for his feet, where Star was lying. He opened his eyes and saw stars in the night sky above him.

"They should be able to find you something to eat in

the servants' hall," Lady Dunkeld had said. "And some bedding. Off you go."

In his potting shed nest of blankets with Star beside him, Archie was soon warm. His bag was tucked under the bench and the basket from Ma hung from a nail among bunches of dried herbs and bulbs.

"This is just us, Star," he whispered. "You and me on an adventure."

In the morning, after he had scrubbed himself down at the garden tap and had breakfast in the staff hall, Dunn took him to the garage. He wheeled out a bicycle that looked as if it had already seen a lot of owners.

"Her Ladyship says to take this and go and find your brother," he said. "You're in luck, it's even got a basket to put your dog in. What more could you want?" He spun the wheels and flicked dust from the dented handlebars. "There's any number of army camps round here. Nearest one's Great Pimlow, eight miles north." He pointed. "And north is thataway."

Chapter Seven

There seemed to be a constant coming and going of ambulances at Fivewells, with army doctors in uniform and nurses wearing white flapping headdresses. It seemed that every delivery van in Kent had been brought here and made into an ambulance, with a hood over the top and a space for a stretcher in the back. Archie stayed well away from them while he learned to ride the bicycle with Star in the basket. He'd hoped to go straight off and find Will, but in fact it took him all morning to get Star to see what he was meant to do. The idea was to lean the bicycle against the wall, put Star in the basket, then get on and ride away, but as soon as the bicycle moved Star turned round and round in circles, barking at the top of his voice and trying to escape. Twice he nearly managed it, and Archie had to get off and tip the frame sideways so that Star wouldn't break a leg jumping out. After that he tried tethering Star with the lead, but Star was so determined to get out that he nearly choked himself. Archie sighed. This would take time.

"You needn't think I'm going off and leaving you here," he said. "You'll have to get used to this."

He had an idea when he was back in the potting shed. He had packed Star's favourite things – Master Ted's slippers, a towel, and the pom-pom Jenn had made – and one of Will's socks, which might come in useful for finding him. The basket on the front of the bicycle was attached to the handlebars by two leather straps – the buckles were stiff and a bit rusty in places, but Archie managed to get them undone and heave the basket off. He carried it into the potting shed, lined it with Star's shopping-bag bed, and put his toys in. One of his own socks turned up in the shopping bag, too, so Star must have helped himself to that when Archie wasn't watching. Archie had grinned when he first saw it. That was what Star used to do with Master Ted's boots.

"Try that, Star," he said, and put him in the basket. Star put his paws on the edge, tipped it over, walked out, and went back for a sock. After that he was willing to stay in the basket so long as it was on the ground, and sideways.

The next morning Archie could hardly stand up. Every fall from the bike seemed to have left bruises. Wincing,

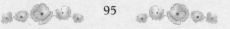

he reached into his bag for the letters his dad and Lady Hazelgrove had written about Will. He wanted to get away, swooping along the Kent lanes looking for his brother, but it seemed that he'd have to be patient.

"Let's try again, Star," he said. This time he fastened the basket to the bicycle, lined it with Star's bedding and toys, and sat Star in it.

"Stay," he said firmly and wheeled the bicycle up and down the paths, rewarding Star with scraps left from breakfast. As he'd hoped, Star was soon more interested in the food than in what the bicycle was doing.

"What about a run on the grass now, Star?" said Archie at last. It wasn't easy to wear Star out, but at least he'd be more likely to sit quietly in the basket if he wasn't bursting with energy. It was another warm day, and Archie walked up and down the paths as Star galloped ahead, sending blackbirds flapping indignantly into their trees.

Archie was impressed. Everything in the Kent garden was two weeks ahead of Yorkshire. He could understand why Will had loved it. And it seemed cruel that Master Ted would never come here to his sister's house and eat peaches from the walled garden, or play cricket on the lawns. It was all wrong, this war. Far away, a man in a blue uniform was walking on two sticks, with a nurse beside him. Archie looked away. It felt wrong to watch the injured man.

He was keen to be away and looking for Will. He called "Carr!" then glanced round to make sure nobody was likely to hear him and changed to, "Star!" Star, who must have run off some energy by now, followed him back to the potting shed.

"In you go, Star," he said, lifting him into the bicycle basket. "We're off to find Will." He fed him a bit of cold sausage. "Good boy."

Star was happier now he knew that the basket meant food and settled down, his ears lifted as he looked out. When the bicycle began to move he whimpered and scrabbled about, but Archie didn't stop. Star put his paws on the edge of the basket, looked down, and saw that it was a long way. He'd have to sit still and make the best of it. Soon, he'd forgotten that he was moving at all.

It was a long ride up and down hill – mostly down – by the time Archie saw the row of tents and huts at Great Pimlow Army Camp. Star was used to this now, and enjoying it. He sat up with his paws on the edge of the basket, looking from one side to the other and occasionally barking at a rabbit. When Archie dismounted and wheeled the bicycle he thought of jumping down, but looked over the edge of the basket and decided to stay put for the moment.

Archie had been expecting to see a few lines of tents but Great Pimlow was the size of a small town, with rows and rows of huts. There were soldiers marching in time with rifles over their shoulders, and another group lying behind a heap of sandbags firing at targets. How could he find Will in all this?

He wheeled the bicycle past yards of barbed wire

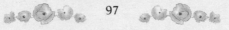

to the main gate of the camp. Two sentries in muddy-coloured battledress had already seen him, and were standing at the gate with their guns in their hands. Archie thought that maybe he was meant to hold his hands up, but he needed to hang on to the bicycle.

"If you've come to join up, son, you look too young to me," said one of them. "Come back when you're eighteen. Tomorrow will do."

"I haven't," said Archie. "I haven't come to join up."

"Nice dog," said the other. He had ginger hair, thin at the front, and put his hand out for Star to sniff. The first soldier ignored Star.

"Now, son," he said. "I have a name, and you use my name when you talk to me. My name is 'sir'. Now, if you don't want to be a soldier, what are you doing here?"

"I'm here to find my brother, sir," said Archie. "He joined up a few weeks ago but he's only fifteen. I've got letters about it, sir."

The "sir" soldier took the letter with an unpleasant smile on his lips, and Archie knew that sort of smile. Bullies looked like that when they were about to pick on you in front of your friends. But he hadn't come all this way to be put off by a school bully in a uniform.

"That'll be a letter from your ma, then?" he said with a smirk.

"No, sir, from Lady Hazelgrove of Ashlings Hall."

"Oh, I say, Lady Hazelgrove from Ashlings Hall!" repeated the soldier in a high-pitched voice. "And who might she be?"

"Lady Dunkeld's mother, sir," he said. "Lady Dunkeld from. . ."

The mocking expression vanished. "I know where Lady Dunkeld comes from!" snapped the soldier. "Does she know about your brother?"

"Yes, sir, he used to work for her."

The soldier glared at him, swore quietly, and snatched the letter. "Stay there," he ordered, and turned to the ginger-haired soldier. "Corporal, if he moves, arrest him. On second thoughts, don't bother. Just shoot him. What's your brother's name?"

"Sir, it's Will Sparrow, but. . ."

"Will Sparrow, or 'but'?"

"Will Sparrow, sir."

The soldier muttered something about being more trouble than the blooming German army and stamped away to the nearest shed. When he was out of the way, the ginger-haired corporal came to talk to Archie. Star was sitting up with both front paws on the edge of the basket, so Archie lifted him down.

"Carr, sit," he ordered. "Stay." Star sat obediently, and stayed at Archie's side.

"Don't mind the sergeant, he's always like that," said the corporal. "He won't get on the wrong side of Lady Dunkeld, her husband owns this bit of land. Does your dog bite?"

"No, sir, he's dead soft," said Archie, who liked the corporal. Star was wagging his tail so he liked him too, which was a good sign. "Only I reckon my brother must have changed his name so we couldn't find him. He

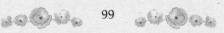

could be called anything. He might have used Taylor, because that was my ma's maiden name, or Carr after the family."

"What does he look like?"

"Bit taller than me sir, bigger frame. Same colour hair. Big hands and feet, sir."

"Could be any of 'em."

Soldiers ran out from one of the huts and stood in ranks. Archie peered towards them, but he couldn't see Will. He scanned the camp, watching every soldier who appeared, but Will wasn't among them. The sergeant was striding back to them. Star, who had been sitting quietly at Archie's heel, came to stand in front of him.

"No Sparrows in this camp," he reported. "No starlings, no swallers, no blooming blackbirds neither. So just fly away before the cat gets you."

"The lad did say his brother might be using a false name, sir," said the corporal.

"Oh, did he? Well, young Sparrow, do you know how many men are in this camp?"

"No, sir."

"No, you don't. Let me tell you, it's getting up to twenty thousand and if you think I can hunt through them all looking for one lad, you're mistaken. He'll have to take his chances with the rest of them."

"With your permission, sir," said the corporal, "perhaps the lad has a photograph of his brother?"

"We never had one done, sir," said Archie.

"And you say he might have called himself Taylor or Carr? Sir, perhaps I can have a quick nosy at the

100

register, see if we've got a Taylor or a Carr come in within the last few weeks? Just as it's a lad that worked at Fivewells, sir, we could make the effort."

"Five minutes, corporal," said the sergeant. But there were no Carrs in the register, and the only Taylors were men in their thirties. They tried the Smiths, too – the corporal said they had an astonishing number of Smiths – but they were all older men, too.

"If I see a lad that looks anything like you, I'll send a message to Fivewells," said the corporal at last. "Best I can do. Your dog didn't like the sergeant, did he? He was standing guard over you."

Archie said goodbye and wheeled the bicycle back to the main road, then lifted Star back into the basket. "I'm supposed to be looking after you, not the other way round," he said. "You're a brave dog, you. Maybe I was stupid to think our Will would go to the nearest army camp to Fivewells. First place anyone would look, and he wasn't going to make it that easy. He doesn't want to be found."

Going to Great Pimlow had been mostly downhill, so the journey back was up. Archie's legs, unused to cycling, were tired and beginning to stiffen. Pushing the pedals was hard and painful, and to his shame he had to get off sometimes and push it uphill. By the time he reached the gates of Fivewells he was aching, hungry, and thirsty. He took Star from the basket but kept him on the lead, because a lorry was coming the other way. A red cross was painted on its side. More of them were parked outside the house, and nurses were hurrying out from the front door. Archie took the bicycle back to the shed, gave Star a drink, and went to the staff hall in the hope of something to eat.

"It's Cook's day off, and I'm not here to get tea for a garden boy," snapped a kitchenmaid when he looked into the staff hall. "Or your dog. You can wait until staff dinner at eight." But just as Archie's stomach seemed to turn to stone, the housekeeper in her neat dark dress bustled into the room.

"You're the boy who's looking for his brother, aren't you?" she said. "Come with me. You can bring the little dog."

The housekeeper's room was smarter and neater than the parlour at home and more comfortable, too. Soon Archie was eating bread and butter and cake and just managing to use polite manners though he wanted to devour the food like a wolf. There was hot tea, too, and "I can always find a few scraps for a doggy," said the housekeeper, and presently the boot boy brought some cold mutton and potatoes for Star. Archie relaxed. The chair was comfortable, the housekeeper was kind, Star was fed and watered and lay contentedly, his head on Archie's foot. . .

Brisk firm footsteps rang along the corridor. Somebody was clapping hands for attention.

"It's Her Ladyship!" said the housekeeper, and sprang to her feet. Lady Dunkeld was marching through the servants' quarters.

"We need stretcher-bearers!" she shouted. "And people to fetch and carry! We need strong arms!"

Archie jumped up. "May I leave S . . . Carr here?" he asked.

"Of course you can," said the housekeeper, smiling down at Star. "He's a nice dog. I remember when Her Ladyship's brother used to come, he had one like it. It must be a Yorkshire breed of dog, is it?"

"Aye, he's a real Yorkshire dog," said Archie and hurried out to see what he could do to help, though he found he was so stiff that he was walking astride, the way Flora did when she'd wet herself. He nearly collided with a nurse.

"How can I help, miss?" he asked.

"We're going to have a house full of badly injured men and they need to be kept warm," she said. "We need fires lit in every room and plenty of logs to keep them going. Can you do that?"

"Logs is this way," said the boot boy, darting past like a terrier. Archie followed him and found that when he arrived in the main hall with an armful of logs there was no need to ask which way to go. From every room, army doctors and nurses called, "In here with the firewood!", and as soon as one fire had taken light and the log basket had been filled he sped away for more wood, forgetting that he had been tired and hurting because now he was doing something vital, now he was making a difference to war-scarred officers. He couldn't help Master Ted, but he'd help somebody like him.

"You're keen!" remarked a doctor as Archie pushed logs on to a fire and sparks flew up the chimney. It must have been his seventh or eighth trip up the stairs when somebody put a hand on his shoulder and said, "Stand back a minute. Stretchers coming through".

Archie stood back so that stretcher-bearers could carry wounded men into what used to be the dining room and was now a ward. This time he couldn't help looking. He couldn't help seeing the man with bandages almost covering his face and the deep red stain, as big as Archie's hand, soaking through. On the next stretcher there was no trace of blood, but the blanket was flat where the man's legs should have been. Men who could walk were being helped up the stairs, some of them smiling bravely and even joking, though their eyes were desperate with pain and Archie had to turn his face away from the bloodstained dressings. Somewhere a man was talking, wildly, too fast.

"They're still falling," he was saying, and Archie saw a man on crutches with a nurse on either side of him. He was wide-eyed and shaking. "Where's Nicholson? Where's Nicholson? Is he dead? I have to write to his mother. They're still shelling! Nicholson! What happened to Nicholson?"

The nurses led him away. The man behind Archie put a hand on his shoulder.

"It gets some of them like that," he said. "War's a noisy business. Especially this one. If you meet any of them around the grounds and they're having an attack like that, try to keep them calm, talk gently, and bring them to one of the staff. Off you go with your firewood."

*

When all the fires were made up and the log baskets full, Archie went back to the housekeeper's room where Star sprang up at him in delight. He had been sitting by the door, said the housekeeper, alert to every footstep as he waited for Archie.

"Good lad," said Archie. "Time to get you outside."

He took Star for a long walk in the grounds. He needed to be in the fresh air, away from the house full of bruising and blood. He threw sticks and Star brought them back joyfully, thrilled with the game which, at this minute, was all he wanted in the world. He loved Archie.

Archie threw another stick. So, he thought, that's what the soldiers look like when they first get here. That's when they've already been to a field hospital. What do they look like when the shell hits them? When they're scraped up from the mud? Will thinks it's all swords and horses like in the stories, and shooting the way Dad shoots rabbits, one shot and it's over. But it isn't like that. It wasn't like that when Master Ted . . . he shook his head. He mustn't think about Master Ted's death.

He made a promise to himself. It would not be Will. Will wouldn't come back looking like that.

He was tired. Even Star seemed to be slowing down.

"St. . ." he began, and changed it to "Carr! Heel!" He was just in time, as Lady Dunkeld came round the corner.

"Carr!" said Archie. "Carr, heel!"

Star found Archie's heel and sat beside it, looking up at him. Then he rolled over to scratch.

"What a nice-natured dog that is!" said Lady Dunkeld. "It was a great shame about Ted's little mongrel. I was fond of that dog, I would have liked to keep him. By the way, did you find your brother?"

"No, my lady."

"Try Amberhurst, there's a camp there. It's a long way, but you're young and healthy, you'll manage it. Cycle through the town and take the left turn at the crossroads, then keep going. If you fall in the sea you've gone past it. If you don't find him there there's always Littledown and Overton. Good hunting!" She looked down at Star. "I rather wish I had one like that."

It would mean an early start in the morning. He walked back to the potting shed, slowly so he could look out for weeds and pull them out as he went along. He turned for a last look at the house, hoping that the men in their beds were comfortable, with clean dressings and something to take the pain away.

He whistled for Star, though he didn't need to as Star was close by and ready to follow him to the shed. It was a way of saying what he felt at that moment – *this is my dog. He comes to my whistle.* Lady Dunkeld had said that she "would have liked to keep" Star. More than ever, she mustn't know who he was. If she did, she could claim him and he couldn't do anything about it. She was Ted's sister. He was just the gardening boy. But he was the gardening boy who was everything to Star just now, as Star was everything to him. They went everywhere together.

He opened the door and Star ran straight to the blanket, scraping and pulling at it.

"Settle down, you daft pup," said Archie. "We have to get going sharpish tomorrow. Let's find our Will and get home."

But they didn't find Will at Amberhurst the next day, nor at Littledown the next. The journey to Overton was so long that by the time they reached Fivewells the great cast-iron gates had been locked.

In rage and disbelief Archie shook at them. For miles he had been thinking of the shed, and a place to lie down, and nobody had told him that they locked up at night. He tried climbing, but the gates and walls had been built to keep intruders out. He might have been able to manage it on his own, but not with Star to hold on to, and there wasn't even room for Star to wriggle underneath. There was nothing to do but to huddle under his jacket for a cold night that seemed to last for ever. He had half a bread bun in his pocket and gave most of it to Star.

The next time they had a long journey to a camp he made sure to pack his bag with food, water, Star's bowl and the blankets from the shed. It turned out to be a very good thing that he did.

It was a normal day for Archie, if a normal day meant cycling for hours through the countryside to an army base and trying to find one underage soldier in a camp the size of a small town. But this time, this one time, the sergeant at the gate took a good look at

Archie, told him to wait, and went to whisper to an officer. Presently he came back.

"This way, son," said the sergeant. "Major Marshall wants to talk to you. You can bring your dog."

"Carr, heel!" called Archie and patted his leg. To his great relief Star stayed at his heel all the way to the tin hut where an officer sat behind a desk. He had a large grey moustache and looked as old as Lord Hazelgrove, and Archie guessed that he was a retired soldier. Archie stood very straight.

"Stand at ease," said the major, who was reading something on his desk. He seemed puzzled when he looked up.

"This is the lad I just told you about, Major Marshall, sir," said the sergeant.

"Oh, yes!" said the captain. "Remind me, your name is. . .?"

"Archie Sparrow," said Archie. "I'm looking for my brother Will."

"May be calling himself Taylor, sir," prompted the sergeant.

"Yes," said the major. "I see. Find young Taylor, sergeant."

The sergeant saluted and marched away. Major Marshall smiled at Archie.

"Jolly nice little dog, that," he observed.

"Yes, sir," said Archie. "We go everywhere together, sir."

"And you're a Yorkshire lad from the sound of it," said the major. "You're a long way from home to be looking for your brother around here." Archie was telling him about Will and Master Ted when the sound of marching feet made him look round.

"Private William Taylor, sir!" said the sergeant, and Archie turned with a lift of the heart, because in a few seconds his search would be over. Will would be angry but that wouldn't matter. He would be safe, that was what mattered, they would go – but he found himself looking into the face of a stranger.

This boy wasn't Will. He was the same sort of build as Archie and a bit taller, and he could understand why the sergeant had thought they might be brothers. But hope drained out of him and left him feeling tired, empty, and even a bit sick with disappointment.

"This isn't my brother, sir," he said. He bent and stroked the top of Star's head to hide his face.

"You're dismissed, Taylor," said the major. The young soldier gave a glance of withering scorn in Archie's direction and marched away.

"All the same, sergeant," said Major Marshall, "ask Taylor a few questions. He looks jolly young to me." He looked up at Archie. "Better luck next time."

"Sorry I've wasted your time, sir," said Archie, because he liked the major and the sergeant who had taken time to help him.

"Not at all. I hope you and your dog find him. Sergeant, see young Mr Sparrow out."

He had seemed so close to finding Will, and now he was back to the beginning again, and the ride home was long. Maybe he was being a little careless, or maybe there was nothing he could have done about it, but one second he was making good speed along a straight road and the next there was a jolt that sent the bicycle lurching sideways towards the roadside hedge. Archie threw himself forward to protect Star, and then there was nothing but earth and sky spinning around him.

The hedge broke his fall. When the dizziness stopped he picked himself up, grimacing a bit because he was badly scratched by thorns, and whistled for Star. From somewhere near his feet came a bark and he looked down to see Star half in and half and out of a ditch, scrabbling with his front paws to get free. Archie reached him, limping a bit, pulled him out, and ran his hands over the thick coat.

"You all right?" he said. "Reckon you got off easier than I did. Let's see. Stand still. All in one piece, Star? We've been right lucky, then. Where's the bicycle? Star, sit. Stay."

The bicycle lay in the road. Archie picked it up and examined it. Master Ted had taught him how to ride a bicycle, and had once shown him what to do if the chain fell off. The chain was still on, but the front tyre was flat. Master Ted hadn't told him what to do about that.

"Long walk then, Star," he said. "With luck we'll be home before dark."

But after many miles of walking it became clear that they wouldn't be home before dark at all. By this time he was carrying Star, and the sky was fading. He knew he couldn't risk being out in the open after dark, with not even the lights of a cottage to guide him. When he reached a village he recognized, he worked out that he was about an hour's walk from Fivewells.

"What do you reckon, Star?" he said. He wanted to press on, to get back to the shed, not to be locked out for another night. But the countryside could be pitch-black within an hour. The village church had a roomy porch where at least they would be sheltered, so he made his way through the churchyard with its old grey stones.

"It's like camping out, you and me, i'nt it, Star?" he said as he spread the blankets on the floor of the porch. "Look what I brought from Fivewells for you!"

There were cold sausages and bread rolls and Archie gave Star the sausages, thinking it was a long way from the chicken and liver he had eaten at Ashlings. But Star gobbled the food down, and they shared the water and curled together at last on the hard floor.

Lying on the cold ground wrapped around Star, Archie thought he'd never get to sleep. He must have drifted away at last, though, because he fell in and out of dreams where wounded soldiers rose out of a hedge and asked him for help, and he was looking for Master Ted, not Will. He dreamed that he saw Will, and Will was in danger and he couldn't warn him . . . he woke up, gasping with relief because it was only a dream after all.

Where was Star? He sat up. There was no warm dog beside him.

"Star!" he said softly.

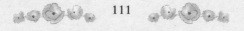

There was a soft sound outside, a sound like brushing or scuffling. He called Star again, but there was no answer. In the dark, fear clutched at Archie.

"Star, come!" he ordered sharply, not because he was cross with Star but because he was afraid for him. Why on earth had he decided to stay all night in this place with the dead in their graves all round him? If they *were* in their graves. He imagined the men and women of Kent rising from their graves, restless because of this war, looking for their sons and grandsons who had marched away to France . . . the ghosts of dead soldiers, unable to rest in their graves in France, coming home to their own villages . . . what if they found him? What if they found Star?

Something growled. Archie held his breath. His heart beat so hard that he could hear it. A sweat of fear broke over him. That was Star's growl.

"Star!" he said. "What have you seen?"

His hands trembled as he wrapped a blanket round his shoulders and crept from the porch. Star was still growling, and he put his hand down to find the top of the dog's head.

"What, Star?" he whispered, crouching beside him. "What is it?" But his eyes were adjusting now. Kneeling by Star, he saw the gleam of eyes in the dark and smelt the sharp stink of fox. He almost laughed with relief.

"Is that all?" he said. "A fox? Were you warning it off? You're a good lad."

Ghosts! It seemed ridiculous now, and he was glad that nobody had been there to see him shivering with fear and fearing the dead. It was a good thing Will didn't know about that. He was still cold, and getting hungry, but he was tired enough to drift off to sleep again until sunrise woke him.

"Hey up, Star," he said, stretching stiff cold limbs. "Let's get to Fivewells for breakfast."

He would have gone straight to breakfast but the officer who always talked about Nicholson was running round the grounds shouting, so Archie went to find the doctor. Together they calmed the man down and left him in the care of a nurse.

"You're the lad looking for his brother, aren't you?" said the doctor. "There's a camp at Charhurst Common, have you tried that one?"

"Haven't even heard of it, sir," said Archie wearily.

"Long way and only a small camp, but worth a try," said the doctor. "Other side of Amberhurst, you'll see it signposted from there. You look exhausted."

"My bicycle's wrecked, and it isn't even mine. . ." he began, and soon he was telling the doctor all about the day before, and their crash, and sleeping in the church porch. "I sometimes. . ." He was tired, and disappointed, and was thinking things he hardly dared to think. "I sometimes wonder if I'll ever find him. He don't – doesn't – want to be found."

The doctor sat on a bench and indicated the place beside him for Archie.

"War confuses things," he said. "They call it the fog of war. People aren't accounted for, there are misunderstandings and mistakes. Everything muddles up. He's out there somewhere. When you find him, give him time to tell you where he's been and what he's been up to. Working here, I find that most soldiers need a good listening to. Just at the moment I'm more concerned about you. I need to have a word with the housekeeper about you. Good meal and a hot bath."

"I need to tell Lady Dunkeld about the bicycle," said Archie. "And I want to feed my dog."

"I'm sure one of the ground staff can sort the wheel out," said the doctor. "And the housekeeper can find something for your dog to eat. Spare him the hot bath."

He felt better for food and a bath, and just for knowing that in this house of troubled men somebody cared about the garden lad. In the evening, Dunn the chauffeur wheeled the fixed bicycle to the shed, grinning, and told him to try not to wreck it again. By morning, Archie felt ready to start once more.

Chapter Eight

Star was scratching at the door and scampering about. He wanted to be outside.

"Go on, you lummox," said Archie, and opened the door. Star cocked his leg against the nearest fence post, then bounded up to one of the patients who was walking in the grounds. Archie pulled some clothes on and went after him. The patient, who was making friends with Star, straightened up and saluted.

"Shell landed on the trench, Captain!" he said, then he began to tremble and his eyes widened until the whites showed all round. "Bad show!"

Archie looked round for help. The kindly doctor was coming out from the house, and Archie waved to catch his eye.

"You're all right now," said Archie. "Here's someone who can help you."

The patient turned, saw the doctor, saluted, and began again. "Shell landed on the trench, sir!"

"Stand at ease," said the doctor calmly. "Let's go and find a stretcher-bearer, shall we?" He led the shaking officer back to the house, glancing over his shoulder to speak quietly to Archie. "Thanks for helping. You look better for a good night's sleep."

"I feel better, sir," he said. "Thank you." He was refreshed now and felt that he was on an adventure to rescue his brother, not just trailing up and down hills on an old boneshaker. It was as if he were the older brother, not Will. After a hurried breakfast he helped himself to some bread for later, filled a bottle with water, and wheeled out the bicycle. The letters from Dad and Lady Hazelgrove were in his pockets, and he lifted Star into the basket.

"Other side of Amberhurst, Star," he said. "Let's find him this time."

A year ago in Ashlings the traffic in the streets had mostly been horses and carts. Only the Carrs, the doctor and the solicitor had motor cars. Here in Kent motor ambulances passed him all the time bringing wounded soldiers from Dover, and army lorries brought soldiers to the troop ships at Folkestone. Archie nearly pedalled straight into a lorry full of soldiers. There was no getting away from the war.

He stopped in a village when his legs refused to cycle any further, even though the church clock told him it was too early to eat. The sun was strong, and sweat made his shirt stick to him. There was another long ride, another break after which getting on the bicycle again was almost impossible, and finally he freewheeled down the hill to see the huts and tents of an army camp sprawling in a valley.

"There it is, Star!" he shouted. He got off and wheeled the bicycle to the sentry post.

"Archie Sparrow," he announced to the sentry who challenged him. He was a stout, solid man, older than most of the soldiers Archie had seen. "I've come for my brother, sir. He's joined up and he's underage."

"Another one, eh? His name?"

"Will Sparrow, sir," said Archie, and prepared himself for a few more jokes about sparrows. He must have heard them all by now.

The sentry walked stiffly to a hut, jerking his head for Archie to follow. A lot of other soldiers in the hut jumped to their feet and tried to look as if they hadn't been lounging about chatting. The sentry leafed through a register while Archie leaned the bicycle against the door.

"Sparrer? No sparrers, not even a spuggie."

"He could be. . ."

"Calling himself something else, I know. It's what most of 'em do, if they think anybody could be bothered to come looking for them." He sat down heavily on a stool and nodded at Star. "What's that, your dinner?" Then he grinned, took a half-eaten biscuit that was lying on the table, and gave a bit to Star. "He's a nice dog, that. Have you brought him to sniff your brother out?" He didn't wait for an answer. "I've got a brother, a dog with a good nose could smell him three streets away. Then again, so could anyone. Blimey, a dog with no nose at all would know my brother was coming, feet like rotten eggs on a hot day. Don't suppose you know what your Will might be calling himself?"

"Could be Taylor or Carr, sir, but it could be. . ."

"Could be anything, same old story. Now, son, I'll tell you. I've fought in more battles than you've had hot potaters, son, and a war's no place for a kid. It's the kids in this country we're fighting *for*. These young lads joining up, most of 'em are more trouble than they're worth. Three months to train up, then a week at the Front and they'll be crying for their mothers, or what's worse, dead. If your brother's here I don't want him going to the Front any more than you, so let's see what we can do. What makes you think he's here?"

Archie told him about Will working at Fivewells, adding "and I've tried all the other camps round there already." He described Will as well as he could, and the sentry puffed out his cheeks and shook his head.

"Could be any half-baked country boy. Let's go and have a walk round the camp, see if you can spot 'im. Me mates here can cover sentry duty just in case the blooming Kaiser turns up. Keep a tight lead on your dog, mind, there's lads practising on the rifle range and you don't want 'im shot." He shook his head again. "Kids! Your brother's not the first and he won't be the last. We had a twelve-year-old last week, twelve-year-old, Lord help him, no bigger than a rabbit. Put his helmet on and couldn't see out of his eyes. What did you say your name is, Sparrer, was it Alfie?"

"Archie."

"And I'm Corporal Hick. But if you want to go on calling me 'sir', I won't object." He led the way to a square like a school playground where soldiers were learning to march, counting out loud. "Do you see 'im among this lot?"

"No, sir."

It was the same at the shooting range, too, and at the training ground where men with bayonets ran roaring at stuffed dummies. In hut after hut, Corporal Hick bellowed "Will Sparrow!" through the door and looked to see if any head turned. Will wasn't in the infirmary, either. The camp was vast and the more Archie saw of it, the more his heart sank. This might be a small camp, but you could still disappear in it if you wanted. His legs began to ache. The sun burned the top of his head.

"Country boys, you and your brother," observed Hick. "He might be looking after horses. Worth a try." He led the way to a stable block where Star raised his head and twitched his nose at the animal smells. Then a stable door opened, and Archie was looking Will in the face.

For a second, nobody moved. It took Archie a moment to recognize Will in uniform, with his hair cut short. Will seemed too astonished to move. Then he dodged past Archie and fled.

Corporal Hick shouted an order and at once every soldier in the camp seemed to be running to seize Will.

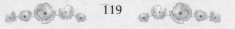

While two of them held his arms, Hick strolled calmly over.

"Will Sparrow? No need to panic, son," he said pleasantly. "Let's go and see your friend the commanding officer, shall we?" And as they marched away, Will turned to glare at Archie with fury.

The camp's commanding officer sat behind a gleaming wooden desk. He looked like Lord Hazelgrove but older. Will faced him, his feet apart and his hands behind his back, with a soldier on either side. Archie and Corporal Hick stayed by the door with Star at Archie's feet while the officer read the letters from Ma and Lady Hazelgrove.

"Will Sparrow, I admire your courage," he said at last. "I honestly do. But I don't send boys into battle. There are plenty of ways a lad like you can serve his country, and this isn't one of them. You're learning to be a gardener. It's a good thing to do. Growing food, that's a real job. Soldiers can't fight without food. Give a gardener a patch of ground and a handful of seeds and he'll feed you through the winter. Be a gardener. Be a good one. When you're older, when we've won this war, the men will come home hungry, and how are they going to eat if nobody's left to grow potatoes? Go back to. . ." he looked again at the letter and raised his eyebrows in surprise. "Have you come all the way from Yorkshire?"

Will said nothing.

"Please, sir. . ." began Archie.

120

"The lad would like permission to speak, sir," said Corporal Hick, and Archie explained about Ashlings, and Will going to work for Lady Dunkeld. At the mention of her name, the officer raised his eyebrows.

"From Fivewells?" he said. "How did you get here from Fivewells?"

"On a bicycle, sir."

"And you, Will?"

"Walked, sir."

"My word, they breed 'em tough in Yorkshire," said the officer. "Corporal!"

"Sir!"

"Take them away – may as well feed 'em while they're here, then find a junior officer who can drive a motor car without hitting a tree and get them back to Fivewells. And their bicycle. And the . . . good gracious, whatever sort of a dog is that?"

The word "dog" alerted Star. His ears lifted.

"We don't know, sir," said Archie. "His mother was a poodle, sir."

The soldiers both laughed, and Archie turned red.

"And his father was goodness knows what," said the commanding officer. "Jolly nice little chap, whatever he is. Will, you've proved that you have courage and you're willing to serve your country, and that's enough. You've got a good brother there. Go on, the pair of you, make yourselves scarce."

Will turned his face away from Archie. He said nothing all the way back to Fivewells.

*

When Will and Archie reached Fivewells, Lady Dunkeld was outside talking to one of the doctors. At one moment, they were climbing down from an army truck. The next, Will was pinned against the side of it with Lady Dunkeld gripping his shoulders.

"So you're back, you wicked little tyke!" she barked at him. "Have you any idea of the trouble you've caused? You lied to me, your parents have been frantic with worry, your brother has come all the way from Yorkshire to find you, what have you to say for yourself?"

"I wrote to my dad and ma, my lady!" gasped Will. He could barely get the words out, and Lady Dunkeld loosened her grip a little.

"Oh, so that makes it all right, I suppose!" snapped Lady Dunkeld, then glanced at Archie. "They didn't get a letter, did they, Archie?"

"No, my lady," muttered Archie wretchedly, knowing it would only make things worse.

"I just wanted to fight for my country, my lady!" protested Will.

"Don't answer me back, boy!" She let go of him so quickly that he staggered, but she ignored him and turned to the driver. "The king, Lord Kitchener, the army, the navy and the what-you-may-call-them, the flying chaps, they can't win the war, you know, not without help from Master William Sparrow." She turned back to Will. "You're a brave lad, I'll give you that. You're also a complete idiot. I'm going to telephone Ashlings and let them know you're here and in one piece. I suppose you'll have to stay here until we get you back to your parents. Make yourself useful. Do some digging or something. You'll have to sleep in the shed with your brother. And I want an apology out of you for being more trouble than you're worth."

"I'm sorry, my lady," he said sullenly.

She began talking to the driver again. Nobody seemed bothered about what Archie did, so taking Star for a walk in the grounds would be a good idea.

"Come on, then," he said, and let Star run ahead. Now and again Star would stop to make friends with a bandaged soldier sitting on a garden bench then he'd race far ahead again and suddenly, Archie felt unbearably lonely. He didn't belong here. Nobody would notice if he wasn't here at all except Will, and Will hated him now. He thought of Dad and Ma, and summer evenings playing cricket on the lawn.

He had Star, and he and Star were everything to each other – but if Lady Dunkeld worked out that Carr was really Star, she'd want to keep him. Star's life was woven into his now, and they couldn't be separated. He threw a stick, and when Star brought it back Archie sat down, took the dog's collar, and pulled him into his arms.

"Stay, Star," he whispered. "Stay. We need each other."

He heard boots on the path behind him, and glanced round. It was Will. Archie turned his face away. Will hadn't wanted to speak to him before. He could be like that, too. A rabbit hopped across the lawn and Star wriggled to be free, so reluctantly Archie let him go. He

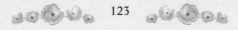

ignored Will until Will kicked him in the hip, not hard enough to hurt much but enough to let him know how he felt.

"Pleased with yourself?" asked Will. Archie shrugged. He didn't know what to say, so he didn't say anything.

"That looks like Master Ted's dog."

"Well, it isn't."

"Get up, you," ordered Will. Archie did, and faced him at last.

"What did you want to do that for?" yelled Will. "Why did you have to interfere? I was doing well, I was training, I was a soldier!"

"Ma's been worried sick about you!" Archie shouted back. "She never knew where you were, Lady Dunkeld thought you were home – if she hadn't said anything, Dad and Ma would have thought you were still here!"

"I told you, I told that officer, I wrote to them! Are you calling me a liar?"

"I'm not calling you anything, I'm saying they never got any letter! What was I supposed to do, stay home and let you get killed? Somebody had to come and find you! And anyway, you *are* a liar, you lied to Lady Dunkeld, you lied to the army, you're a liar, you're a cheat. . ."

Will grabbed Archie's shirt. He was shaking with anger. "I'm not a coward like you!"

"I'm not a coward, and get your hands off me!"

"You never tried to be a soldier! Cowardy, cowardy. . ."

Archie kicked him hard in the ankle, Will

overbalanced and then they were rolling on the ground, punching and kicking. Barking like gunfire, Star launched himself at them and grabbed Will's sleeve.

"Carr, let him go!" yelled Archie, and remembered the right command just in time. "Carr, *give!*"

Star released the sleeve. The boys sat up, breathless and battered, and Will pulled his sleeve round to look at it.

"He's torn me shirt!" he grumbled. It wasn't really a tear, just a hole, and it had stopped them fighting, but it didn't improve Will's mood. Star ran to Archie's side and sniffed. Archie smelt of sweat, but he wasn't hurt. All the same, he'd watch that boy.

"Got your little dog to look after you?" growled Will. Archie knew that Will was trying to provoke him, so he sat still with one arm round Star.

"Never got any letter," he said. "Honest."

"Well, I sent it."

"Must have got lost," said Archie, and couldn't resist adding, "I'm not a coward."

Will gave him a look as if Archie was such a coward it wasn't worth discussing. And Archie knew there was no point in saying anything more to him just yet.

There was so much he could have told him. He wanted to give news from home, tell him about Dad's bad leg and how Ma, Jenn and little Flora were helping in the garden. He could tell him about the memorial garden they were going to make for Master Ted. Sooner or later, he'd explain about Star. And maybe, when Will had calmed down a bit, he'd see the ambulances arriving and the injured officers and the ones who'd left their sanity behind in the trenches, and understand what Archie had saved him from.

From somewhere in the gardens came a shout, and a man in pyjamas ran across the lawn, his pyjama jacket flapping open. Archie recognized him. This was the officer he'd seen yesterday, shocked and shaking and talking about someone called Nicholson. Seeing Archie, he took him by the shoulders.

"Where's Nicholson?" he asked. Star stood in front of Archie, watching.

"I don't know, sir," said Archie.

The officer looked round and saw Will. "Have you seen Nicholson?" he demanded.

"Who's Nicholson?" asked Will.

"If the noise would only stop, I could think," said the officer. "Nicholson? What happened? Shall I write a letter?" A nurse was walking towards them.

"You want to go with this lady, sir," said Archie. "She'll help you. She'll get you some paper and you can write your letter."

"Nicholson?" he asked once more. The nurse led him away gently by the arm and Will stared after them.

"What happened to him?" he asked.

"What do you think?" Archie muttered back. "The war, that's what." They said little to each other all evening, and to Archie the time seemed endless. Star stayed close to him, and it was a relief to everyone when it was time to go back to the heap of blankets on the potting shed floor.

Star sensed Archie's unhappiness. He stayed very close, and lay down with his head against Archie's leg.

"Don't snore," said Will, but Will was the one who snored and kept Archie awake late into the night.

When he woke in the morning, Will had gone.

Chapter Nine

There was mist on the gardens when Archie ran outside with Star ahead of him. Maybe Will had just gone for a wee, or to the house to see if there was any breakfast going – but the birdsong told him that it was too early for anyone to be making breakfast yet. He ran, calling, then went back to the shed. Will's bag had gone.

"Star!" he said. "Find Will!" Star ran and sniffed, but Archie was pretty certain that he was more interested in all the other scents he could find.

"Star, heel!" he said. He brought the blanket from Will's bed and held it under the dog's nose. "Will! Find Will! Come on, Star, concentrate. Find Will!" He didn't know if Master Ted had ever taught Star about following a scent, but it was worth a try. "Seek! Seek Will!"

He had no idea whether Star had understood or not but the dog ran towards the house, so Archie followed him. It would be all right, thought Archie, he's just gone to the house, he's still here . . . in the staff hall the kitchenmaid was on her knees in the grate, trying to coax the fire into life.

"If you want bread you ask for it," she snapped. "Don't just go helping yourself like the last one did."

"My brother? Was he here?"

"I wouldn't have minded, but he could have helped me get the fire going," she grumbled. "Just helped himself and ran."

"May I have some bread, please?" he said, knowing there was another long journey to come. He couldn't force Will to come back. He'd have to persuade him.

The bicycle was still propped against a wall where Dunn had left it. He clipped Star's lead to his collar and took him to the gate, wheeling the bike with his free hand.

"Where's Will?" he said. "Seek Will!"

Star pulled on the leash to the right and Archie raked his memory for what he had learned about Kent. The channel ports lay that way, where the troop ships left for France.

"Good dog!" He bundled Star into the basket and rode off. Will would be walking, he was on the bike. Depending on when Will had left, there was a pretty good chance of catching up. He rode furiously, leaning forward over the handlebars, almost out of the saddle, looking out for Will round every bend, over every hill. He was riding so fast that when he did see Will trudging along the side of the road he had to stop too quickly and fell off. Star tumbled out of the basket, rolled over, and picked himself up. Will turned quickly.

"Are you all. . ." he began, then saw who it was. "Oh, it's you again." He set off again, walking quickly.

"I'm not going to stop you," said Archie. "I just brought you some more bread. If you're going, you're going. Do you want any message taking home?"

This seemed to make sense to Will. He stopped at last and they sat by the side of the road together, sharing the bread with Star.

"You can't go back to the same camp," said Archie. "They'll only send you home again."

Will shook his head and gulped down a mouthful of bread before answering. "I'm going to Folkestone, where the troop ships go from. I'll get on to a ship somehow, and once I'm in France they won't send me back again. It wouldn't be worth their while to send me back. I'm a trained soldier now."

"Half-trained."

"Shut up."

"Why did you have to join up in the first place?" asked Archie. "You didn't have to."

"There'd be no glory in it, would there, if I only did it 'cause I had to!" said Will. He sat hugging his knees and gazing out across the Kent countryside. "What happened was – I was working for Lady Dunkeld, I was doing all right. I was in town on my afternoon off, and I was looking in a shop window when these three lasses came past. They were whispering. The one of them marched right up to me and gave me a white feather."

"They did that to you!" exclaimed Archie. "Couldn't they see you were. . ."

"No, they couldn't, that's the point. Don't you get it? I felt grand about that! It meant that I looked old enough to join up! So I did."

"Will," said Archie carefully, because he didn't want Will to run off again, "I've seen the men at Lady Dunkeld's hospital. I've seen more than you have, I know what it's like when they come back from the Front. You've already shown that you're brave, you don't need to do any more."

"That's when it's really brave, Archie," he said. "I know more than I did when I first joined up, I've heard them talking about what happens in war. It's no good hearing about wounds and all that stuff and running back home again. Not even if I ended up. . ."

He stopped. Knowing that he was about to say something important, Archie waited. Finally, looking down at his hands, which were tightly clasped, Will muttered, "Like that man in the garden yesterday."

"Oh, him," said Archie. He had thought that Will meant Master Ted, but he was talking about the man who kept looking for "Nicholson". So that was Will feared most, ending up like that. But in spite of that he still meant to get on to a troop ship. He thought he'd never admired Will so much.

131

Star stood up. He looked along the road, growling softly.

"What would we do if you came back like that?" asked Archie. "We'd all have to look after you, Ma and our Jenn would have to wait on you like a baby. You're – you're a right good chap, Will. We need you. It's not about fighting the war, it's about getting the world back together after it. We've lost Master Ted and Frank Roger. We'll need brave people like you alive and well."

In that moment he felt that they weren't fighting the Germans at all. The Germans were probably a lot of gardeners and farm boys too, who fought for their country because they'd been told to. They were fighting against stubbornness, the refusal to listen and understand, whether it came from a gardener's boy or the rulers of countries. At least, that was his battle just now.

"Ma misses you," he said.

"Stop trying to stop me," said Will, and Archie knew, because he'd known his brother all his life, that Will was afraid, very afraid, but his pride would make him go on in spite of it, plodding the Kent roads, looking for a port and a troop ship. And Archie couldn't go back without him. He would have to follow and stay with him because Will needed him, and Ma and Dad and all of them needed him to stick to Will so that at least he could tell them where he was. Perhaps, by the time they got to Folkestone, he'd have thought of some way of getting Will to go home. He could slip away, have a word with an officer or somebody, explain, show the letters – yes, that's what he'd do.

Star was still growling. Will hoisted his bag on to his shoulder.

"I'm coming with you," said Archie.

Will scowled. "Suit yourself," he said.

Archie clipped Star's lead on, looked along the road, and saw why he was growling.

"There's an army convoy coming," he said.

It wasn't an army truck that came first but an ambulance, a large green hooded truck with a red cross on the side, bigger and smarter than the ones that usually turned up at Fivewells. It was followed by a few more army ambulances including one that looked like a converted grocer's wagon. The first slowed down, and the driver leaned from the window to call to Archie. A nurse in uniform sat in the passenger seat, and behind them was a blue curtain to screen the part of the ambulance where the injured men would be.

"Morning, lads," said the driver. "I reckon we took a wrong turning somewhere, how do we get back to the London road?"

Archie hesitated, but Will came to his side.

"Give over, Archie, you'll only get him more lost," he said. "And keep the dog quiet." Star was fascinated, trotting this way and that, and sniffing. Will began giving directions and seemed to know what he was talking about, so Archie led Star away, walking him alongside the line of ambulances. In some of them a bandaged soldier sat in the passenger seat – those were the ones who could sit up, thought Archie. There was

always that curtain between the front of the ambulance and the back.

"Carr, heel!" he ordered. "And be quiet! Quiet!"

Star was agitated now. Maybe there was a smell of battle and blood that upset him. Archie tried to pull him back to the grass verge but Star resisted and barked and a driver glared down at them.

"Sorry, he's not usually like this," muttered Archie and bent to pick Star up, but Star had both front paws against the side of an ambulance. It was as if Archie wasn't there. There was only Star, and the ambulance that so excited him. Archie tried again to pull him away, but Star held fast.

"Come here," he said, and wrapped both arms round Star to lift him away, but with a strong and sudden twist Star leapt free and through the open window. The driver and a nurse grabbed at him but he had already disappeared through the curtain.

"There are patients in there!" shouted the nurse. She jumped down, ran to the back of the ambulance, and opened the doors. Archie was there before her.

"Get that filthy animal out of my ambulance!" she snapped. "What's it doing? Get it off my patient!"

But to Archie, her voice seemed to come from far away. She was on one side of life and death. He stood with Star on the other.

In the back of the ambulance was a single stretcher, with a chaplain in uniform sitting beside it. On the stretcher lay a man covered with a grey blanket. Only his face showed, but that face was so wrapped in bandages that there was just enough room for him to breathe and drink. His one visible eye was closed. Star was on his hind legs with his front paws on the stretcher, tail wagging, whimpering a little. The injured man did not move. One arm lay at his side, with something in his hand.

"Out!" ordered the nurse. The chaplain reached to lift Star away from the stretcher, but Star jumped on to it.

"Get down!" shouted the nurse.

"He won't, miss," said Archie and found that he was shaking because Star was so utterly absorbed, so intent on the man on the stretcher, that it could mean only one thing. And that thing wasn't possible. He leaned down to see what was in the injured man's hand.

Star turned and sat beside the man on the stretcher. He looked up at Archie and barked.

"Quiet!" said the nurse. Star ignored her and barked again.

"Quiet, Star," said Archie. "Shh, now."

The driver leaned round to speak to them.

"Sort yourselves out back there," he said, "we're ready to go."

"Out of there, our Archie," called Will.

"This is our Master Ted," said Archie. "Star's found him." He turned to the nurse. "This is our Captain Carr. We heard he was dead, but this is him, miss. The dog knows."

Will had found his way to the back of the ambulance to see what the fuss was about.

"Don't be so daft, our Archie," he said. "Master Ted got killed. You know that."

"Look at Star," said Archie, forgetting to change Star's name. It wouldn't matter anyway, in front of these people who didn't know about him. "And look at this. They were wrong about Master Ted."

He lifted the hand that lay on the grey blanket. The nurse tried to stop him, but the chaplain shook his head at her.

"It's a cross," said the chaplain gently. "He's been holding on to it all the time."

"It isn't, sir, it's a sword," said Archie. He wriggled it free a little. "It's got his initials on it. Look, sir, for Edward Francis Stephenson Carr. That's his name."

"This man was found with no identification at all," said the chaplain. "No tags, nothing with his name. Are you sure about this sword? We thought those initials must be a regiment. East-something-something Corps."

"I made it for him, sir. And his dog knows him, you can see that."

"You could be right, our Archie," said Will.

"Does he look like your Master Ted?" asked the chaplain.

"He doesn't look much like anyone, sir, not with all those bandages," said Archie. "But that's him." He looked at Star, lying with his paws on the blanket, his eyes bright with joy as he stared at the still face.

"Well then, your Master Ted is on his way to hospital," said the chaplain. "They'll do their very best for him."

"He has to go to Fivewells, sir," said Archie. "It's near here, it's his sister's house, but she's made it into a hospital. That's where he has to be."

The chaplain and the nurse looked at each other without speaking. The driver looked round again.

"We're holding up the whole blooming convoy," he grumbled. "We could have built him his own nursing home by now."

"It's a proper hospital with doctors and wards and everything," said Archie.

"He's right, it is," put in Will.

The chaplain was still looking at the nurse. He spoke softly.

"I think he could go to his family, don't you?"

"Yes, I think so too," she said, and now she wasn't snappy at all, only quiet, and Archie heard what they weren't saying. Master Ted was so badly injured that it wouldn't matter where he went.

"Will, get on t'wheels," he said. "Ride ahead and. . ."

"I'm off," said Will, and for a second Archie thought that Will would just jump on the bicycle and pedal hell for leather to Folkestone and the nearest troop ship, but he could have done that while they were all talking about Master Ted, and he hadn't. He disappeared round the bend in the road, on the way to Fivewells. As the rest of the convoy headed for London, Archie gave the driver directions to Fivewells then knelt down beside the stretcher.

"Master Ted," he said. "Can you hear me? It's Archie. Archie Sparrow the gardener's son. You're going

137

to get well. Your Star found you, it's like you've been given back to us and we're going to get you better. We're going to your Julia's house."

He stroked Star. "Well done, you," he said. "Good boy."

By the time they reached Fivewells Lady Dunkeld was waiting outside the house with two nurses and a doctor. The second the ambulance stopped she opened the doors. Her eyes looked puffy and he guessed that she'd been crying, but she took control as if she were a general with a stick under her arm.

"Ted," she said firmly, "Ted, it's Julia. You're at my house and you're going to be as right as rain. Nurse, come with us. Have you got his notes? Where's Will Sparrow? Will, run round to the staff hall, tell them I want my own bed made up for him. Archie, move your dog."

Star allowed Archie to lift him down, but he still watched Master Ted. Archie wanted to help with the stretcher, but they didn't need him.

"I need to telephone Mother at once," announced Lady Dunkeld. "And, Archie!"

"Yes, my lady?"

"Well done. Good man. We'll look after him now. Off you go."

Chapter Ten

It seemed to be hours before Archie fell asleep that night. Star scratched and whined at the door until only exhaustion made him sleep.

"I know, Star," said Archie softly. "I don't like being shut out, either. You and me and Master Ted, we should all be in the same place." He wanted to be with Master Ted, talking to him about Ashlings and willing him to live, putting his hand on Star's head. "But it's all down to his family now, not me."

Before breakfast, he went to the servants' hall with Star dashing ahead and Will trailing reluctantly behind them. The kitchenmaid was stirring porridge.

"Any news of Master Ted?" asked Archie.

She glanced up and jerked her head towards the

staff corridor. "You have to go to Housekeeper's room," she said. "The pair of you."

The housekeeper in her neat black dress was waiting for them with an anxious little frown on her face. The boys stood with their hands behind their backs like timid schoolboys while Star hunted desperately and whined at the door. The housekeeper gave him a biscuit but he ignored it, scratching at the door and hoping to find Master Ted.

"Quiet, Carr," said Archie, but Star was too agitated to take any notice.

"Lady Dunkeld left very early this morning," said the housekeeper. "She left instructions about you. Will, she said it was time you saw your family again."

In spite of everything, Archie had to look down to hide a grin. Will wasn't looking forward to facing his family. Star put his paws up on Archie's knees to tell him to open the door.

"And Archie," she went on, "you've found your brother, so there's nothing to keep you here. You are both to go home today. Lady Dunkeld very kindly left money for your train fare."

"But please, ma'am," said Archie, "can't I stay here with Master Ted?"

She looked puzzled. "Master Ted? Oh, do you mean Captain Carr? Lady Dunkeld took him with her." As Archie gawped at her, she went on, "Her Ladyship really is most resourceful, and very determined. They left at first light in one of the ambulance vans. Her

Ladyship thinks the poor boy should be at his own home, where his mother is."

Archie's heart leapt with hope. "So has he woken up?"

"Oh my dear, no," she said gently. "These are bad times, and we have to prepare for the worst. Your Captain Carr may never wake up. That's why she was so urgent about getting him back to his mother."

The express train was a shining dragon flying them home in clouds of steam. Archie and Will shared the compartment with two soldiers on leave and a woman who knitted all the way from King's Cross to York. It was a quiet journey, as Will said as little as possible and Star slept most of the way while fields, villages, towns and stations disappeared behind them and Archie looked out of the window saying silent prayers for Master Ted. At last the train steamed and screeched into York and it was time to change to the engine and two carriages that huffed and rambled across the moors to Kirby Moss.

"We might be in time," said Archie as the whistle blew. "Master Ted might be all right."

Master Ted had to be all right. If he died now, all of them, all the Carr family and everyone at Ashlings would go through that grief again, and how could they bear that? At least if he came round long enough to know that he was home and in his own bed . . . and if Star could be with him. . .

. . .and Star had to be with him, Archie knew that.

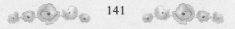

He was Master Ted's dog, and Master Ted needed him more than Archie did. Archie had fed and cared for Star, and they had explored the wilds of Little Keld Wood and the long roads of Kent together, shared food and curled up together for warmth at night. But with all his heart Archie wanted Master Ted to live, and if he lived he must have his dog back. The price of Master Ted's life was this. Archie would have to part with Star. Somehow, he'd have to bear it.

The light was fading when they walked through Ashlings village to the Hall and past it to Gardener's Cottage. There were lights on at the Hall, and the curtains were open.

"He might still be alive," said Archie. "We could go and ask."

"Do you have to go on about that now?" snapped Will, and Archie realized that he and Will had been in different worlds all day. All he could think of was Master Ted and Star. For Will there were Dad and Ma and Lady Hazelgrove to be faced, and Archie knew now that he must be dreading it. He must have faced sergeant majors often enough, but now he was bracing himself to meet his own family. For the first time, Archie wondered what Ma would say to Will.

The door was unlocked. They stood in the kitchen doorway with their caps in their hands. Ma was folding the washing.

"Hang your coats up," she said without looking up. Star ran to greet her, and Dad slowly folded the newspaper he was reading.

Ma bent to stroke Star, and looked at them as she stood up. From her face Archie couldn't tell if she wanted to hug Will or hit him, and then he realized that she didn't know either. Jenn, in her nightie, was leaning over the banister to watch. The awkward silence was making Archie's toes curl but Will spoke at last.

"Sorry, Ma. Sorry Dad. I did try to tell you. I wrote. I didn't want you to worry."

With a shake of her head and a cry of "What am I to do with you?" Ma strode across the floor, hugged Will tightly for a second, then held him at arm's length and slapped the top of his head.

"I should wallop you," she said, but she didn't. And Dad looked past her at Archie, gave the slightest nod of his head, and said quietly, "Nice work, son."

Archie nodded back. Nothing more was needed.

"Sit down, lads, while your ma makes a brew," said Dad. "Will, you and me will have a talk int' morning. Our Archie, Her Ladyship sent a message for you. You're to go to the Hall tomorrow morning sharpish, she wants to see you."

"Any news of Master Ted?"

"The word is he opened his eyes once or twice, just a bit, and shut them again. He's still with us." Then he took Archie firmly by the shoulders and spoke in a way that Archie had never heard from him before, as if he were afraid of crying.

"You got him home, son. You got our Master Ted back to his own."

"It was Star that found him," said Archie, and bent to bury his face in Star's fur.

Star still wanted to find Ted, but for the moment he was content to be in a place he knew and liked. He had found Ted and would find him again and wake him up. Meanwhile his water dish was where it should be, and there was a bit of soggy toast on the floor that Flora had dropped. The room smelt of Archie and Ma and Dad, Jenn and milky puppy Flora. It was an Ashlings place. It would do for now.

In the morning Archie left Star at Gardener's Cottage and went to the Hall. Lady Hazelgrove's eyes looked pink and wet and she looked about to cry all the time, so that he felt awkward and didn't know where to look. Lord Hazelgrove had come home when the news about Master Ted had reached him, and he and Lady Hazelgrove sat straight-backed in their armchairs asking Archie for every detail of what had happened when he found Master Ted. He told it as well as he could while leaving Star out of it for now. If Ted lived Lady Hazelgrove would have to know that he and Dad had disobeyed her orders and kept Star, but he wasn't ready to talk about that yet. Connel came to sniff curiously at him but Lady Hazelgrove called her back and she lay elegantly at Her Ladyship's feet while Brier and Sherlock sprawled beside His Lordship. Lord Hazelgrove looked much older than he had before he went away to train soldiers but they both looked kindly at him, so kindly that he dared to ask for what he wanted so much.

"Please, my lady, my lord," he said, "please, may I see Master Ted?"

"It would only be right," said Lady Hazelgrove. "Come with me."

He wished he'd remembered to put his Sunday boots on. It felt wrong to walk up that grand wide Cinderella staircase in his gardening boots and there were so many doors he wondered how the Carrs ever managed to find their own bedrooms, but at last Lady Hazelgrove stopped and opened a door. He turned his head away from the smell of staleness and disinfectant, then pulled himself together and took a good look at where he was.

The big, simple room was at the end of the first floor with two windows, one overlooking the lawn and the other facing west. Master Ted's bed was near the end window. A big ugly dressing table was at one side of the room with a big ugly wardrobe at the other, and a smart writing desk stood by the south-facing window. There was a little round table, a chair, and a bookshelf. A nurse sat knitting in an armchair beside the bed where Master Ted lay looking much too pale and still.

There was no dressing on his head now and an ugly purple scar ran from his hairline across his left eyebrow and down to his ear. Deep grey-blue shadows were under his eyes. His right arm lay on the covers, and Lady Hazelgrove took it in hers.

It took a minute for Archie to realize what looked

so strange, so unfinished about Master Ted. Then he knew. Where Master Ted's left arm should be, the blanket was flat.

Lady Hazelgrove bent over her son.

"Ted," she said, "Archie's here to see you. Archie Sparrow from the gardens. He's the one who found you and took you to Julia." She looked round at Archie. "He might still be able to hear, so we keep talking to him. We've played him his favourite music on the gramophone, too, haven't we, Ted? He needs anything that will reach into his brain and wake it up. Come and talk to him."

Archie stood by the bed but his mouth was dry, and there was not a word in his head. Even on his own he wouldn't have known what to say. With Lady Hazelgrove and the nurse there, it was hopeless.

"What should I say, my lady?" he asked.

"Anything," she said. "Tell him about your family. The gardens. Julia said you had a dog with you. I didn't know you had a dog. Tell him about that."

Of all the things . . . he swallowed hard.

"Master Ted, it's Archie from the gardens," he began. "My lady says to tell you about – about the dog. He's the best. He's as fast as an express train, sir, and dead nosy. Daft as a brush, sir, always after rabbits and never catches one. And he thinks everybody's his friend – well, maybe everyone except our Will. He's a mongrel with smudgy patches and – and I called him Carr after the family." He was running out of things to say, so he finished, "anyway, you have to get better and see the gardens. It's strawberry time and there's still some asparagus. Wake up and you'll get some. And, sir, it'll be the Dawn to Dusk cricket match soon. You always captain our team."

He knew he'd turned red. That was such a stupid thing to say to a man who'd lost one arm that he only wanted to escape.

"Please may I go now, my lady?" he asked.

"Of course, Archie. Thank you."

He walked back to the house very slowly, kicking a pebble. When he got there, Star was asleep in his basket. He looked as if he'd always lived in Gardener's Cottage and always would.

Archie squatted down beside him. Star opened his eyes slowly, saw Archie, and scrambled to his paws.

"What about a walk, then?" said Archie, and Star's tail wagged furiously. "What about a run? Let's hide you in the barrow and go to the wood!"

Under the shelter of the beech trees in Little Keld Wood Archie picked up a stick to throw. Star watched, bright-eyed and excited.

"Now, Star," said Archie. "We'll have the best time ever."

They walked for hours that day, they ran, they splashed in and out of the beck. Archie climbed a tree, called Star, and watched the dog looking for him, but he couldn't bear to leave Star confused for long so he dropped down to be greeted like a long-lost best friend. Then he threw sticks into the beck, and when Star ran in to fetch them Archie ran in too, and rubbed water through the sooty smudges on Star's coat. After Star had shaken himself dry he found some good soft mud to roll in so Archie had to wash him again, and then made sure that they stayed on the high dry ground. At last, when every last stick had been found and shaken and carried about, every squirrel chased up a tree and every rabbit put to flight, Archie whistled for Star. Star trotted to his side. He was content.

Archie clipped the lead to Star's collar and walked him back to the cottage, wheeling the barrow at the same time. It was all over now. If anyone recognized Star, it wouldn't matter.

At Gardener's Cottage, nobody was home. When Star had had a drink Archie did his best to clean off the rest of the smudges with soap and did so well that only faint traces remained. After getting so wet the dog looked unusually clean, and his coat was soft as a puppy's. White hairs drifted into the air when he moved. Archie sat down beside him.

"We've got to be right big about this, Star," he said. "We've got Master Ted back now, and you found him. You're a good dog." At the sound of Master Ted's name and "good dog", Star's ears lifted. "He's your master and you have to go back to him. He's not well, and you can help make him better. You understand? You're a grand dog. If it were up to me I'd never—" he swallowed hard, then went on "—I'd never part with you ever, not for all the world and everything in it. And I have to explain it all to Lady Hazelgrove and she's going to kill me, but you don't have to worry about that."

He was glad nobody was there. He wrapped both arms round Star, pressing his face against him. Then drew his sleeve across his eyes and fastened the lead again.

"Come on, Star," he said. "Let's find him."

As it turned out, Archie hardly got a word in. He stood in the Great Hall with Star at his feet. Star's tail was wagging, but Archie's stomach felt the way it did on the drive to Kent in Lady Hazelgrove's car. Then Lady Hazelgrove was there with Connel beside her and Star was straining at the lead.

"Archie!" she cried. "Is this. . ."

"Yes, my lady."

"But it can't be!"

"It is, my lady."

"Star!" she called, and Archie couldn't have held on to the lead if he'd tried. Star hurled himself at Lady Hazelgrove, jumping for joy, wagging his tail and falling over at her feet. Connel looked down from her great height, tail wagging slowly in welcome as Star ran round in circles and finally crouched in front of her with his face between his paws and challenged her to a play fight. Lady Hazelgrove lifted Star in her arms and held him, lifting her face as he tried to lick her.

"It's really him, isn't it!" she said. "It's Ted's Star!"

"My lady, I'm very sorry," faltered Archie. "I can explain. It's not my dad's fault, it's. . ."

"Archie, stop," she said firmly. She put Star down, but she still watched him with a soft, kind smile, the way people smiled at little Flora. "Since Ted was found I've blamed myself every day because of Star. What was I going to tell Ted if he came round and asked for his dog? And here he is!" She put a finger to the corner of her eye. "Little Star. I've missed you. It's quite wonderful, it really is."

"Please, my lady, I just couldn't stand to see it done," he said. "So. . ."

"Quite right too." She knelt to stroke Star and smooth his long ears. "So was it Star that you had with you at Fivewells?"

"Yes, my lady, but Lady Dunkeld didn't know. It was really Star that found Master Ted, my lady."

"And he can find him again," she said, and stood up. "Thank you, Archie. With all my heart, thank you. Let's take Star up at once. Star, shall we find Ted?"

"Star, seek your master," said Archie.

Star bounced up the stairs with his ears flapping and flew along the landings. Outside Master Ted's room he barked insistently.

"Quiet, Star," said Archie.

"Let him bark," said Lady Hazelgrove happily. "Ted needs to hear him. You've no idea how good it is to see him bounding along like that! He's settled straight back in as if he'd never been away."

"Yes, my lady," said Archie, but the words were dull in his mouth and heavy in his heart. He shouldn't have given Star an order at all, not when Lady Hazelgrove was there. The door opened and Star hurled himself at the bed.

"Down!" shouted the nurse. "My lady, I'm so sorry, a dog in the. . . Shoo! Bad dog!"

"It's all right, nurse," said Lady Hazelgrove. "Let him be. This is Ted's dog and if anyone can make Ted better, he can."

Star jumped on the bed, sniffed, and wondered why Ted didn't wake up. There were strange sniffs around him, very clean and not quite right, and he was catching a whiff of something unpleasant that reminded him of the vet. Poor Ted, had they taken him to the vet? He still smelt like Ted, though, and tasted like him too.

"I would prefer not to have the dog licking the patient's face, my lady," said the nurse sternly, but it was too late.

"Ted," said Lady Hazelgrove, "it's Star. Your little dog, you remember? You'll have to wake up now."

Archie took Master Ted's right hand. The nurse tried to stop him but Lady Hazelgrove simply said "nurse" in a voice nobody would argue with. He placed the hand on Star's head and stroked the stiff fingers down the dog's back, head to tail. Star twisted round to have a lick.

"It's your Star, Master Ted," he told him. "He wants you." Then he left Master Ted's hand on Star's head.

Taking Star back had been the right thing to do, the only thing to do. He'd only been looking after Star because they thought Master Ted had died. But taking him back had seemed impossible, and he couldn't quite believe that he had found the strength to do it. He almost wished that he hadn't. Now he looked down at

Master Ted, still and silent with that scar on his head and his hand over Star, who looked as bright-eyed as any dog could, and he found he was smiling. Forgetting where he was and who she was, he turned and beamed up at Lady Hazelgrove, and she smiled back and put her hand on his shoulder. *I can do it now*, he thought. *It won't be easy, but I can walk away and leave Star here.* He looked back at Master Ted and gasped.

They all saw it at the same time. Master Ted's fingers were moving. His eyes were still shut, his wrist did not move, but his fingers flexed, stretched, and curled into Star's coat.

Behind them the door opened. Archie didn't turn, but the firm step told him that Lord Hazelgrove was here. For a moment he thought he'd have to explain about Star all over again.

"Good gracious!" said Lord Hazelgrove. "I thought that dog was dead!"

"Archie did something quite marvellous," said Lady Hazelgrove. "And, look! Look at Ted!"

"Good gracious!" he said again. Soon Master Ted's hand lay unmoving on Star's back.

"But he did it!" said Lady Hazelgrove. "He moved! We all saw it!"

"Let's not get our hopes up too much," said the nurse.

All the way back to Gardener's Cottage Archie relived that moment when Master Ted's fingers had moved, and he smiled whenever he thought of it. But all the same, it was a lonely walk. That night he lay awake in a strange quiet with no Star to lie on his feet, or sigh in his sleep.

"You crying?" asked Will.

"Shut up," said Archie.

The next morning, work had to go on as normal. Archie took the vegetables to the kitchen and walked into a hubbub of chatter from the housemaids.

"He must have meant Miss Julia. . ."

"Or Caroline, maybe he meant Caroline. . ."

"Why would he talk about her, he never sees her. . ."

"He meant t'nurse, didn't he?"

"Who meant what?" asked Archie, handing over the basket.

"Master Ted!" said Aggie, almost jumping with excitement. "He opened his eyes and said something. Mr Grant was there and he said it wasn't very clear but it might have been 'sister', so I reckon he meant t'nurse."

"Maybe he's lost his memory, poor soul," said somebody else. "If he's lost his memory he might think he's a little lad again, and he wants his sister."

A wide grin spread across Archie's face.

"That's daft," he said. "He meant 'Star'."

"Oh, yes, the little dog," said a housemaid. "I wondered what had happened to him. We thought he'd died. That's what we heard. He's up there now like a blooming hearthrug."

All the way home the news shone inside Archie. Star had done it, he had called Master Ted back from

that deep dark place of trenches and death. He was proud of his – of Master Ted's dog. In his head, he said it again. *Master Ted's dog* – and it seemed as if just thinking of the dog made him appear, because Star was galloping across the garden to him while Lady Hazelgrove followed with Connel. Archie dropped to his knees and soon Star was in his arms, wriggling as Archie ruffled his coat.

"Hello, you!" said Archie, and for a moment it was as if nothing had changed, as if they were running about Little Keld Wood again. Star shook himself free, found a stick, dropped it at Archie's feet and scampered back, watching for the throw.

"Morning, my lady!" called Archie. "I hear Master Ted's started to talk!"

"Isn't it splendid news?" she said. "Star, come here and stop pestering Archie. Poor Ted, he'll have to learn things all over again."

Star brought back the stick and Archie threw it again. "Please may I go to see him, my lady?" He felt quite at ease with Her Ladyship these days. But a small, slow smile told him the answer before she said anything.

"Not yet, Archie, he needs to keep quiet. And you know, he won't want people seeing him when he's still not quite right. I'll tell him you asked after him."

"If you ever want Star taking for a walk, my lady, I'm most willing to," he said.

Lady Hazelgrove gave that little smile again, the sort of smile she would never use to a member of the family, only to staff. "I'll take Star out with Connel, just as it used to be," she said. "Dear Star, he's easily confused – he has to learn all over again that he lives at the Hall. We're most grateful to you, you know, for all you've done."

And that was that. There was nothing to do but give a nod of understanding, pat Star, and go back to whatever the day's tasks were. He'd been shut out and put in his place. The gardener's boy.

Just once, he looked over his shoulder. Star was watching him. Then Lady Hazelgrove called, "Star, heel!" and he trotted reluctantly after her.

All the rest of that day, Archie tried not to think about Star, and the more he tried, the harder it was. Days passed, and he was astonished to find that he'd been without Star for a whole week. Fivewells seemed like another world.

On his afternoon off he wandered into the village and found that Sam the Boots had a free afternoon and was there too. They bought barley sugars and sat on the church wall together, eating the sweets and kicking their boot heels against the wall, and talked about Will running away to the army.

"He said he sent a letter," said Archie. "It never came. But things like that happen in war time. The doctor at Fivewells told me about the fog of war. Things get mixed up."

"When do you reckon this letter were meant to come?" asked Sam.

Archie thought about it. "Dunno," he said. "Maybe

end of March, beginning of April, I reckon. About the time we heard about Master Ted."

"Our Harry were helping at post office then," said Sam. "They didn't let him do the telegrams, just the letters, with him being new. He asked me one day about Gardener's Cottage, 'cause he was meant to take a letter there and he didn't know where to find it. He said he gave it to one of the gardeners in the grounds to pass on to your dad. That big chap. Harry said he were a surly old beggar."

In Archie's mind, pieces began to fit, to move and fall into place. He thought of Bertenshaw, angry at Dad for getting him sacked.

"Reckon we should get home now," said Sam.

"It were Bertenshaw," said Archie, staring ahead of him, and in his heart he felt a rage that he had never felt in all these months. The worry Ma and Dad had been through, the endless traipsing round the countryside looking for Will, all because Bertenshaw had stolen a letter. "He did it out of spite for our Dad."

"You reckon?" asked Sam. When Archie didn't answer, he went on, "Mr Bertenshaw's two lads got killed. Everyone said he didn't care for them, but he's gone to pieces since he heard about them. He was doing some work on the roads, but now he just does enough to buy drink. He's always in the Fox and Geese."

Archie still said nothing. The rage was too strong. He wanted to do something, not talk or listen. His fists clenched and unclenched.

Then he thought of all he had done these last weeks, and all he had learned. He had made journeys that would once have seemed impossible. He had found Will, and Master Ted, and made a sacrifice that still stunned him. And all that time, what had Bertenshaw done?

"Archie, let's get home," said Sam, and Archie went with him. They kicked pebbles and fir cones all the way home, and were nearly back when two gunshots came from the grounds.

"Someone's having rabbit pie tonight," said Sam. "Or pigeon. Pigeon pie. The air feels thundery today, reckon we might have a storm."

From the house came a terrible scream and a volley of barking from Star. Archie forgot everything and ran in at the front door of the Hall.

Chapter Eleven

He was halfway up the grand staircase before he realized that he shouldn't be there at all, but he couldn't stop. All he could do was run to Master Ted's room, and behind him came the quick tap-tap of a lady's shoes. From Master Ted's room came another scream and a crash. Archie knocked and ran in without waiting for an answer.

Star was scampering away from the door, his tail between his legs, and ran to Archie. The bed was empty, with the nurse kneeling beside it.

"Captain Carr," she was saying firmly, "are you listening to me?"

Master Ted was curled underneath the bed, shaking. His knees were drawn up and his arm over his head to cover his ears.

"Up you get, Captain!" said the nurse. "Pull yourself together!"

Archie knelt beside Star to stroke and soothe him. The dog was trembling under his hand. Broken china lay in a pool of water on the floor.

"Out you come," said the nurse, but Master Ted didn't seem to hear her and she caught sight of Archie. "Out, boy!"

She could have been talking to him or to Star, but they both ignored her. With a swish of skirts, Lady Hazelwood came in.

"What on earth is going on?" she demanded.

"Just a few little gunshots outside, my lady," said the nurse. "Captain Carr got very agitated. He was getting out of bed and shouting, and the dog got excited so he barked, which made it a lot worse, and Captain Carr was in such an overwrought state that he picked up the water jug and threw it across the room. I think he was aiming at the dog."

Archie held Star more tightly. Lady Hazelgrove swished across the room and sank down by the bed.

"Ted, my dear," she said. "What's the matter?"

Master Ted was shaking so much that his teeth were chattering. The whites of his eyes showed.

"Calm down, Captain Carr!" ordered the nurse.

"Please miss," asked Archie, "are you an army nurse?"

"Lady Hazelgrove!" exclaimed the nurse. "Do I have to put up with this boy?"

Lady Hazelgrove wasn't listening. She was still

talking to Master Ted. Archie put down Star and lay on the floor beside the bed.

"Hello, Master Ted," he said gently. "It's all over now. You're not at the Front. This is your bedroom. Take a deep breath. Here's your ma . . . your mother. You'd best come out slowly so you don't hit your head on the bed."

Master Ted stayed where he was.

"You don't have to come out if you don't want to," he said. "It's just, you're lying on a hard floor there and it's not very comfortable. But if you want to stay, I'll stay too."

He twisted round to talk to Lady Hazelgrove. "Please, my lady, there were lots of men like this at Fivewells. They'd had too much war and it got right inside their brains, and Master Ted's had a head wound as well. It's not surprising he's all – you know—" he searched for the right word, and found the one that Ma used for everything from a little sadness to raging misery and anger "—upset. There were men at Fivewells got upset like that, my lady." He turned back to Master Ted.

"There's no guns any more, sir. Look, here's your mother. And the nurse. And here's your dog. Your Star. He's scared. You mustn't throw things at Star, sir."

At last, with a bit of help from Archie, Ted crawled out and sat on the bed. He was still shaking.

"So s-sorry," he said, stammering through trembling lips. He frowned as if something troubled him. "Do you work here?"

"Yes, sir, I'm Archie from the gardens."

160

"Archie?" He smiled the smile that would always be a little crooked now. "Is that your dog?"

"No, Master Ted, he's yours."

"My name's Ted. Ted. Just Ted. Call me Ted. What's the dog called?"

"Star, sir." At the sound of his name Star stood up hopefully.

"Star, stay," said Archie. Ted, as he supposed he must call him, was still in a terrible state and he'd already thrown the water jug.

"I think I just behaved very badly," said Master Ted. "So sorry. Mother – nurse – what's your name again?"

"Archie."

"Archie. So sorry. Simply shocking headache. Not that that's any excuse."

"It's all right, Ted," said Lady Hazelgrove gently, sitting on the bed. "We understand."

"Pardon me, my lady, but we don't," said Archie. "We don't understand, do we, Ted?"

Ted shook his head miserably.

"So we need you to explain, sir," said Archie. "We need you to tell us about it, then we'll understand a bit more."

"Excuse me!" snapped the nurse. There was a crackle, which Archie supposed must be the starch in her uniform, as she stood up. "My patient must not be distressed! He must not even think about his memories, let alone discuss them! He's been to the Front, he doesn't have to bring it home with him!"

"Nurse, may I have a word?" said Lady Hazelgrove,

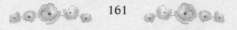

and the two of them left the room. Presently Lady Hazelgrove came back alone. The room was stuffy and there was a thundery heat in the air so Archie opened a window.

"They should have left me there," muttered Ted. "Why didn't they? Why did they have to save me?"

"Because you were worth saving," said Lady Hazelgrove. "What would I do without you?" She seemed to have forgotten Archie, but then Star scampered to the door and sat beside it looking hopeful. "Archie, the dog wants to be out, would you take him, please? And on your way out, would you ask them to bring tea up here for Master Ted and myself? And Archie. . ."

"Yes, my lady?"

"I closed that window for a reason. The sound of guns, you know. Loud noises upset him."

"Yes, my lady," said Archie. "Come on then, Star."

He didn't have to tell Star twice. Star trotted beside him, staying close and looking up at him as if he needed Archie to tell him everything was all right.

"Little Keld Wood then, Star?" he said. "That's our place."

By the time they reached the wood, Star seemed to have forgotten what had happened. All he wanted to do was fetch sticks.

"It's like it used to be, Star, you and me going out in't wood," he said. "Poor old Mas— I mean, Ted. He's like the men at Fivewells. I've seen more than Her Ladyship has, I could help him. But they're the Carrs of Ashlings and I'm the gardener's son, and that's that and all to do about it."

He threw a stick. "We're all the same to you, aren't we?" he said. Star didn't care if you were a lord or a lad, so long as you looked after him. It should be the same for Ted, too.

There was still some creamy white meadowsweet and pale yellow honeysuckle in the wood, and Archie cut some to take to the Hall when he took Star back.

"Are those for Master Ted's room?" asked Mr Grant. "I shall take the dog upstairs and the flowers, too."

"But Mr Grant, can't I go up myself?"

"He needs quiet," said Mr Grant. "I'm sure you have things to do."

Star followed Grant up the stairs, but at the top he turned and looked down at Archie. There was nothing Archie could do but walk away with his eyes prickling.

That night, the thunder broke. Jenn and Archie stood at the window watching as rain hammered and bounced from the ground and swept in sheets across the window. Water sluiced down the paths.

"Dad'll be right cross," said Archie. "It'll bruise the soft fruit."

"It'll spoil the roses an' all," said Jenn. "Look, Archie! There's somebody out!"

Sam the Boots was running across the lawn, wrapped in a coat much too big for him that flapped round his ankles. Water sprayed up around his feet.

"He's coming here!" said Archie, and ran down to

open the door. Sam arrived out of breath with water dripping from his hair.

"For pity's sake, Sam, get in and shut the door," said Ma. "And get your wet boots off before you catch your death."

"Her Ladyship sent for Archie," said Sam. "She wants you at the Hall, now. Master Ted's. . ." he glanced at Ma, "having a bit of a turn."

"Archie, get your coat," ordered Ma. "If you can do anything for Master Ted you'd better get going. Sam, give me those socks and put some of Archie's on, you're staying here until this rain stops."

Ted was curled up under the bed, shivering, his arm over his head. Lady Hazelgrove knelt beside him and Star lay cowering in his basket with his ears down. At the sight of Archie, he ran to his side.

There was another crash of thunder. Ted convulsed and cried out.

"Get down!" he screamed. "Get down!"

"Lord Hazelgrove can't bear to watch this," said Lady Hazelgrove. "The nurse was only making it worse. She's used to old people and invalids, but I don't think she knows anything about soldiers. He won't let me touch him. I've tried talking to him, but I don't think he can hear me."

"I don't know what else to do, my lady," he said, sitting down on the floor beside them. "I suppose it's best to keep talking to him, all t'same. Better than not hearing anything except thunder, my lady. I'd best give him a pillow and his blankets."

With a lot of crawling about under the bed, Archie managed to make a sort of nest for Ted. Lady Hazelgrove hunted through the bookshelf.

"The *Just So Stories*," she said. "He loved this book when he was a boy. The one about the elephant was his favourite. He liked *Treasure Island*, too. I wonder if they would help?"

So as the thunderstorm and rain battered the house, Lady Hazelgrove and Archie sat on the floor taking turns to read to Ted until at last – it seemed like Archie to hours – he seemed to remember where he was, and came out, and allowed them to put him to bed. The rain had stopped. Finally, Archie turned to Star.

"It's all right," he said gently. "Good dog. He's just not himself." He looked up at Lady Hazelgrove. "Shall I take him out once more before Mr Grant locks up, my lady?"

He took Star round the grounds, then back to the staff hall to dry his wet paws. Back in Ted's room he ordered Star to his basket, but Star watched him all the time. When Archie said goodbye to Lady Hazelgrove and was about to go home, Star tried to follow him and Archie's heart hurt for him.

"You have to stay, Star," he said gently, smoothing Star's ears. He lifted the dog and sat him on the bed at Ted's feet. "Look after him. Goodnight, Master Ted, I mean Ted. Goodnight, my lady."

"Archie?"

"Yes, my lady?"

"Kindly come back in the morning."

"Yes, my lady."

Star settled down on the bed and laid his head on his paws. He understood. He must take care of Ted, who seemed to have stopped throwing things.

The next day Lady Hazelgrove reorganized everybody. Will was not to go back to Lady Dunkeld. He was to stay and help Dad so that Archie would be free to help her look after Ted, who might still have difficulty in walking for some time. She had "spoken", she said, to the nurse, who left at the end of the week.

Often a sudden loud noise would send Ted diving under the bed again, so Archie or Lady Hazelgrove would talk to him or read. They worked their way through all Ted's boyhood favourites – *The Jungle Book, Treasure Island,* and something called *Fifty Adventure Tales for Boys* which was full of stories of young men riding horses, climbing mountains, and fighting with swords. Then just when Archie thought he'd lose his voice if he read any more, Ted began to talk. At first he didn't say much, but in time he talked about trenches, mud and shelling, limbs blown off and thundering guns, fire and light in the sky and the screams of men and horses. Star would lie across Ted's feet to comfort him but his eyes would be on Archie. Ted talked about long thirsty marches and falling asleep on his feet, the men he helped and the men he couldn't help, and the constant mud, cold and shelling. There were the sudden rages when he would throw things or kick the furniture.

"And the guns never stopped," he said, shaking. "Not for a moment. I still hear them in my head."

"But when you hear a bang now, it's nothing," said Archie. "Just somebody dropping a tray or His Lordship doing a bit of shooting. If you go outside you'll get more used to it. You're cooped up in here day after day, sir, and it's not good for you."

On a sunny day, more than a month after coming home, Ted made the long journey down the stairs. Slowly, struggling, Archie and Ted made their way along the landing to the top of the stairs with Ted walking close to the handrail but refusing to hold it. Archie kept in step with him. Star couldn't quite understand about walking so slowly, so he trotted ahead and sat down to wait for them. So long as Archie was there, he felt safe.

A lifetime ago, when war was declared, Archie had stood in the Great Hall gazing up at this staircase. Now he spent more time at the Hall than he did at home. But from the top with Ted beside him, the grand staircase looked more forbidding than it ever had from the bottom.

"I think you'd better hold on to the banister, Ted," he said. Lord Hazelgrove hurried up the stairs to help.

"I'll hang on to you, shall I, Ted old chap?" he suggested, and put an arm round Ted's waist. "Archie, you go on in front of us. If he does fall he'll have something to land on."

Archie didn't see Ted's first steps downstairs. He only heard a sharp gasp of pain and a little muttered swearing, then the sound of feet on the stairs behind him. Lord Hazelgrove was saying things like "steady, now" and "well done". Star, who couldn't do stairs slowly, bounced down and sat at the bottom waiting for them. Lady Hazelgrove watched with Connel at her side. And as Archie walked down with awkward slowness he noticed that more and more people appeared in the hall. Mrs Satterthwaite the housekeeper and one of the maids paused in what they were doing. Mr Grant was there, and footmen appeared from somewhere. Soon most of the household seemed to be in the hall, all standing absolutely still. Star wagged his tail. Archie took the last step, and turned.

Ted's face grew white with effort and his lips were pressed closely together, but at last he stood at the bottom of the grand staircase, and everyone, including Archie, was applauding. Star wagged his tail and led the way to the door.

"Good dog, Star," said Archie. "You can sit outside in the sunshine, Ted."

Mr Grant brought a chair. Ted sat down and squinted into the sun.

"What's over there?" he asked. "Where does that path go? I should know these things, shouldn't I?"

"You've forgotten it all, dear," said Lady Hazelgrove. "It'll come back to you. That's the drive, and the path goes to where the new garden will be." Presently Grant came and whispered to Lord and Lady Hazelgrove, who went back inside.

"Why's the dog doing that?" Star had found a stick and was bringing it back to Archie, who threw it. Ted

watched with interest. When the sound of a *thwack!* came from the grounds Ted didn't tremble, stare, or hide, but he put his head on one side to listen.

"What was that?" he asked.

"Somebody's playing cricket, sir," said Archie. "That was a bat on a ball."

"Cricket?" Ted frowned, and Archie could see he was searching his memories. "Did I play that?"

"You did, sir," said Archie. "You were the best for miles. And you'll play again."

"Don't talk such nonsense," said Ted firmly. "I'm tired. Help me up the stairs."

Archie took him to the foot of the staircase, but he was pretty sure he'd need somebody else to help him climb them. He placed Ted's hand on the banister.

"Hold on, sir," he said. "I'll get somebody to help."

He left Ted there and went to the green baize door which led to the staff hall. When he returned with a footman, Lord and Lady Hazelgrove were coming out from the study.

"Ted mustn't know," Lady Hazelgrove was saying, then saw Ted and stopped.

"Ted mustn't know what?" demanded Ted harshly. "Tell me!"

"My dear," said Lady Hazelgrove, "I'm afraid it's about one of your friends."

Ted's face had already hardened with bitterness. "Who is it this time?" he demanded.

"I'm afraid it's your friend Bettany," she said. "He died at the battle of—"

Ted cursed harshly. His hand on the banister was as tense as a claw.

"Archie, get me up the stairs," he ordered.

It was hard, slow going. Star ran past them and waited at the top of the stairs, but his ears drooped. He followed them to the bedroom with his head and tail down.

"Go," said Master Ted and pushed the door shut so hard that Archie had to snatch Star out of the way. He stood outside the door with Star in his arms.

It might be good for Ted to have Star for company. But Archie couldn't leave the dog with him, not with Ted in this rage.

He sat down on the landing. All that work, all the sunny days spent in that room, and finally one great afternoon – and now it was ruined because of one more stupid awful death in one more stupid battle in this stupid, stupid war. It seemed that they'd never get Ted back, Master Ted, *our* Master Ted. For the first time, Archie wondered if it might have been better if Ted had died in a field hospital far away.

With a jolt, he realized that Lady Hazelgrove was beside him. She looked old and tired.

"Leave the dog with me and go home, Archie," she said. "Come back in the morning and we'll see how he is."

"Yes, my lady." He let go of Star and walked away, his head down. When he realized that Star was following him, he turned.

"Star, seek Her Ladyship," he said.

Star wondered what he'd done wrong and where he

was meant to be now. He followed Lady Hazelgrove miserably.

Late that evening at the cottage, Archie cleared some space on the table. He wanted to spread out the plans for the sunken garden. Gardening would be good for Ted.

"He can learn," said Archie. "He won't be able to do everything, but he has to learn to do loads of stuff by himself. We can all teach him."

Dad gave a wry smile. "Just what I need," he said. "Another apprentice."

That remark reminded Archie of the shortage of staff in the gardens. In turn, that made him think about Bertenshaw.

"Dad," he began – and he told Dad and Ma what he'd heard about the letter. Dad nodded slowly.

"You did right, son," he said. "There's not much left of him now."

"It's Master Ted you need to think about, not that Bertenshaw," said Ma. "How's he getting on?"

"I think we're back to the beginning," he said. "And sometimes Star wants to be with me, like he did just now, and I have to leave him." His eyes prickled. "I gave him back, Ma, and it were hard, were that. But even that's not enough. I have to keep giving him back, all the time. It's right hard, Ma."

Her hand was on his shoulder.

"Keep going, our Archie," she said. "You're doing a grand job there. Just you keep going."

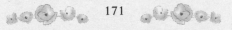

Chapter Twelve

By the next day Ted wasn't angry, but he wasn't anything much. Archie found him sitting at the table in his room looking at a book that he wasn't really reading. His breakfast lay untouched on the tray. Archie put a hand against the teapot. It was still full and barely warm.

There was a pattering of paws and Star ran in. He jumped up at Archie first, then at Ted, and sniffed upwards at the table.

"Aren't you going to eat that, sir?" asked Archie. There was no response.

"It's a shame to waste it. If you don't want it, we'll eat it."

"Help yourself," said Ted without looking up. Archie shared cold sausages with Star, then took the *Just So Stories* down from the shelf. He read until Ted

172

suddenly said, "Shut up, Archie", then he took Star out. After they had run each other exhausted and Star had annoyed a few gardeners, they came back breathless, with windswept hair and fur.

"I don't know how you can stay cooped up in here, sir," said Archie. "Star and I have had a right good run. It's a grand day, and the summer won't last for ever. You need to get out while you can."

Master Ted ignored him. The next day, he greeted Archie with, "What are you doing here? Why aren't you working in the garden?"

"Because Lady Hazelgrove likes me to be with you, sir," said Archie. "And Star wants you to take him for a walk."

Star heard the word "walk" and his tail began to wag.

"You take him," said Ted.

Archie would have loved to take Star for a run in the gardens, but that wasn't the idea. "He's your dog, sir," he said.

Star whimpered.

"That's what I told him, Star," said Archie. Ted made a bit of a face and got stiffly to his feet.

"Oh, come on, the pair of you, if it'll keep you quiet," he muttered.

It was another long slow struggle down the stairs, and as soon as they were outside Star tore around the grounds finding scents that needed to be examined and trees that needed watering. He hunted down the best stick in the garden and dropped it in front of Archie, who folded his arms.

"He's your dog, sir," said Archie.

Stiffly and awkwardly, Ted picked up the stick and threw it. It didn't go far, but it was a start.

"Well done, sir!" said Archie.

"It's all I'm good for," muttered Ted. "Throwing sticks for a dog, is that all I'll do for the rest of my life? You needn't think everything's all right now just because I threw a stick. I still have nightmares. I still get into a lather about loud noises."

"Not as much as you did, sir. You're better than you were. And you'll go on getting . . . you know . . . like you used to be."

"No, Archie, I won't!" he snapped. "You have no idea! Shall I tell you what it feels like? This war took my future away, any fool can see that. But that's not the worst thing. The worst thing is that it's taken my past and cut me off from it."

Archie thought about this. "Do you mean losing memories, sir? Because I think they're coming back."

"But it's as if they're not my memories," said Ted. "It's as if they're nothing to do with me. I can't believe I was ever happy. And then they told me that Bettany's gone. He was the best of us! Betters was twice the man I am. He had brains, he wanted to be a doctor and he would have been, too, if not for this mess. Why am I still here and he isn't?"

Archie didn't even know how to look at Ted because he knew that there were tears in his eyes. He watched Star and finally said, "Will you come with me, sir?"

He led the way to the ferny, stony hollow where

the sunken garden was to be. Not much had been done to it.

"I don't know if this would help, sir," he said, "but when we thought you were dead we wanted to make this a garden to remember you. We'd call it after you so that everyone who came here would think of you, sir."

Master Ted sat down on a boulder and rubbed his left leg, which seemed to be hurting.

"Is that right?" he said, and was silent for a long time. Then he said, "We could make it for Betters, couldn't we? The Arthur Bettany Garden. We could bring his parents to see it. They might like that."

It was what Archie had meant to suggest. But he said, "That's a grand idea, sir" so that Ted would think that it was his idea alone. "You could help, sir."

"We'll talk to your father about it, Archie," he said. "Where's the dog gone?"

Star was having a wonderful time. He had found a ball, which was the best toy in the world. He took it to Archie, dropped it, and shuffled back, waiting for the throw.

Ted picked it up and turned it in his hand. "I've seen a ball like this before," he said, frowning. "Is it a cricket ball?"

"Yes, sir. Aren't you going to throw it?"

Ted threw half-heartedly. Archie could sense Star's disappointment as he trotted over to retrieve it.

"You have to bowl it for him, sir," he said, hoping that Ted's body would remember what to do even if his mind didn't. "You take a run at it."

Ted ran awkwardly and slowly, but he ran with the ball in his hand. And as Archie watched, something changed. Ted was still slow and lame but he was running as if he meant it. His arm stretched and cartwheeled over and the ball flew from his hand. He stood watching Star and flexing his arm, a bit out of breath.

"What happened there, Archie?" he asked.

The grin felt too big for Archie's face. "You bowled, sir, just like you used to. You were the best cricketer in the village."

"I don't remember cricket."

"Your arm does, sir. You bowled overarm. Right proper."

It was a start, but only a start. Archie wished that Ted would suddenly change and become the man he had been before the war. It wouldn't ever be like that. But little by little, Ted came back to life.

There were still days when he said little, even if Archie and Lady Hazelgrove had persuaded him to go outside. In the grimmest and darkest times Lady Hazelgrove would ask Archie to take Star home with him, in case Ted screamed and panicked in the night and scared him. Ted still wanted to know why he was still alive when Bettany and so many of his friends were dead. But as summer turned to autumn, there were fewer long silences. His walking improved. He helped to build the new garden.

"He's loads better, Star," Archie told the dog. "I think we're over the worst. We're a good team, you and me."

He'd never thought that Star was very bright. A year ago, before the war, he'd seen him as an excitable mop that got under everyone's feet. Since then he'd seen how loyal Star was to Ted and to himself. Star had jumped in to protect him from Will when they were fighting. He might look like a mop, but he had the heart of a lion. Star had real sense, too, not intelligence the way humans have it, but understanding. He knew that more often than not it was Archie who fed and walked him. But he knew, too, that Ted still needed him.

There was an afternoon when Archie went home to Gardener's Cottage and found Dad and Ted talking about cricket. Star ran to greet him. Dad had found an old clipping from the local newspaper with a picture of the Ashlings village team when they had won a local trophy.

"There's not much cricketing weather left this year," Dad was saying. "And not many men left to play it. We managed to get a team of old crocks together for the dawn to dusk match this year, but with my bad leg I didn't even get to play in that."

"Just as well I can't remember it," said Ted. "I'll never be a sportsman again."

"Hey up, Star," said Archie quietly. "He's off again. What are we going to do about him?"

With help from Mr Grant, Archie found out that there was a village match the following Saturday. He didn't go to see it himself – there was too much work to be done – but Lord and Lady Hazelgrove and Ted went. Afterwards, Ted told Archie and Will about it.

"I really used to do that, didn't I?" he said. "When I watched it I sort of knew about it. I knew what the batsman was going to do. I knew how the pads feel, and the feel of a bat, too. You need two hands to hold a bat."

"You could do it with one, sir," said Will. "You'll get right strong in that arm now you're helping int' garden." He and Archie were getting on better these days.

"No, I'll never play cricket again and I'm too crocked to stay in the army," said Ted. Presently he marched back to the house with Star following dutifully at his heels, and Archie knew that this would be one of Ted's bad days.

"He really wants to play cricket," said Archie, watching them go.

"Well, he should!" exclaimed Will, "He's born to it. And he's a Yorkshireman born and bred, and a Yorkshireman can play better with one arm better than anyone else with two."

"We'll prove it to him," said Archie.

As the days grew shorter and colder, Will, Archie and Ted were on the lawn on every day that was dry enough. Ted began by bowling badly and batting even worse, but Star loved having so many stray balls to chase. He got to play outside, he had his friends and a ball. What could be better? Dad sometimes joined them and they let Jenn play, too. As she pointed out, she was a good cricketer and with so many men away they couldn't afford to be stupid about not letting girls play. Sam the Boots and Aggie sometimes played, too.

In November there was a letter for Ted from his sister Caroline in Norway. Ted would love Norway, she said. The air was fresh and clean, and would be good for him. There would be nothing to remind him of the war. Soon it was December and there was talk of Ted going to Norway in the New Year.

Archie heard this news and slipped away for a while to tell himself what it meant. Well, he had been through so much already this year. He had already faced loss and sacrifice. Somehow he would handle yet another parting.

As the weather grew colder, a fire was lit in the hearth in Ted's bedroom. Archie thought this was wonderful. So did Star, who sprawled blissfully in front of it. They were there one day when Ted had go downstairs to take a telephone call, so Archie sat on the hearthrug with his arm round the dog.

"Look at this, Star," he said. "That's a grand fire, is that. I hear he's off to Norway, and I reckon he shouldn't go. It's right cold in Norway and that can't be good for him. But I suppose they know how to keep warm." Star stretched and sighed with contentment. "Lady Caroline and her family, they'll know how to look after themselves. I just hope they keep you warm, too. You look after him, mind. You bring him home soon."

At least, he hoped so. It hurt Archie, not just that he would miss Star but that Star would miss him. Poor Star.

"We've been lucky," he said. "Ever since I brought you back here I've been able to take you out. We've had fun. Reckon it couldn't last for ever." Then he added, "I'm sorry, Star," because he knew this would be as hard for Star as it was for him.

Everybody at Ashlings was determined to defy the war by having a good Christmas. Paper garlands were made, kitchens were fragrant with warm spices, and a tall forest-smelling fir was loaded on to a cart and drawn across the estate to the Hall. Will, Archie and the staff planned and organized.

"What if it snows?" asked Dad.

"I hope it does," said Archie.

"Aye, snow would be grand," said Will.

"Daft pair," said Dad.

On the twenty-second of December, thick flakes of snow fell on Ashlings, filling the air and tumbling to the lawns. As long as the light lasted Archie, Jenn and Ted threw snowballs for Star, who chased them, snatched up mouthfuls of snow, and galloped back wanting more. As twilight settled, Ted turned to go home to the Hall.

"Do you want me to come and dry him off?" asked Archie.

"I can manage that myself, thanks," said Ted. "I'm getting pretty good at coping. Star, heel."

"I'll call as usual tomorrow, sir," he said. Star followed Ted slowly, stopping to watch Archie.

The next morning, exactly a year since Master Ted's first homecoming from the war, Archie went to the Hall as usual. Lady Hazelgrove herself was at the door to meet him and led the way up the stairs. In Ted's room, the fire burned brightly in the hearth. Star scrambled up from the rug and ran to greet Archie with delight, putting his paws up and wagging his tail furiously.

"The snow settled beautifully," said Lady Hazelgrove as Archie scratched under Star's chin. "Do come to the window and look."

Ted did as she said. Archie grinned and followed them.

"What on earth. . .?" he began, then he began to laugh, and Archie realized how long it was since Ted had laughed like that, a wholehearted, happy, man's laugh. "They're playing cricket in the snow!"

"It's the Dawn to Dusk cricket match, sir," said Archie. "You missed the one on the longest day, so we're having another one on the shortest. Still dawn to dusk, sir, but shorter."

It was an odd-looking match. There were no cricket whites because everyone was dressed up in winter clothes with boots, hats and mittens. The snow around them had been churned up, but now and again a batsman would send the ball flying far into a drift.

"There's Father!" exclaimed Ted.

"He's captain of the Hall team, sir," said Archie. "And the vicar's captain for village. Some of them are pretty crocked, sir. And my dad's the umpire."

"There's Grant!" said Ted. "And Sam, and there are girls playing!"

"Our Will's playing for the Hall, sir," said Archie.

"And so am I. I'm going in after Will and you're in after me, sir."

Ted turned to him with an expression he could not interpret. For a moment he thought the whole thing was about to go terribly, horribly wrong, and Ted would fly into one of his rages. But then he grinned like a happy schoolboy.

"What a simply marvellous idea!" he said.

"We've set up the Great Hall as a pavilion," said Lady Hazelgrove. "People can come in and get warm. There will be hot drinks and mince pies, then a buffet lunch, and after dark we'll all sing carols."

Star put his paws on the sill and wagged his tail with happiness. *Ted's having a good day! What's going on? They've got a ball!* He gave a soft, gruff bark to tell Ted what to do.

"Where's my coat?" demanded Ted. Archie found it and helped him into it. The left sleeve was pinned neatly across the front. Ted grinned at Lady Hazelgrove.

"I know it's not all over," he said. "I know I'll still have bad times. But today won't be one of them. Star! Up and at 'em!"

So Captain Edward Carr pitched in to the 1915 Ashlings Hall versus Ashlings Village Dawn to Dusk Midwinter Cricket Match. Everyone in the village seemed to have managed a bit of free time to come and watch, and in the Hall the staff looked down from upstairs windows and applauded. Ma arrived with Flora so wrapped up that she looked like a little round bear. Dad said that he didn't know how to umpire any longer because Star and Lord Hazelgrove's dogs were chasing down stray balls and snowballs and even Connel forgot to be dignified and leapt about in the snow like a leggy puppy. Ted was so determined to do well that he hit the ball flying over a hedge and one of the dogs found it and gave it to Lord Hazelgrove. Then somebody else hit it so hard that not even the dogs could find it and Lord Hazelgrove bowled with a snowball, and Dad announced a draw just before the whole thing turned into a snowball fight with cricket bats. As the light faded they all crowded into the hall, boots and hats steamed before the enormous fireplace, and there was punch and hot chocolate to drink. The maids handed round mince pies and shortbread, everyone sang carols, and Star stayed happily at Archie's side.

"It's almost like there wasn't any war," Archie said to Ma.

"If there weren't no war, we wouldn't be playing cricket in midwinter," said Ma. "But it's been a grand day."

By Christmas Eve the snow had frozen. It crackled under their feet as Archie and his family went to the Hall in the pale sunset of late afternoon. There was more carol singing, and the vicar came to lead prayers for the soldiers away in the war and the families whose sons would not be coming home at Christmas. When most people had gone, Ted came to talk to Archie. Star ran a few circles round Archie, then sat down on his feet.

"A very happy Christmas to you, Archie," said Ted.

"And to you to, sir," said Archie.

"You know I'm off to Norway in January," said Ted. "I'll be staying with my sister Caroline for a while. Fresh air, beautiful scenery, all that. Then I'll come home and find something useful to do."

"That's good, sir."

"I couldn't do all that Betters was going to do," he went on, "but I want to help chaps who've had a hard time in the war. And their families. Don't know how I'll do it. Maybe visit in hospitals. Maybe do what you did, just listen and hang around and help them start living again. Thanks for everything, Archie."

"You're welcome, sir."

"Sorry I've behaved shockingly sometimes."

"That's all right. I know how it is," said Archie, surprised at how grown-up he sounded. "All the very best then, sir."

"And, Archie," he said. "I have to think about Star. He's had a confusing time lately, don't you think? And he wouldn't fit in with Caroline's household. She's very fond of cats, you know."

At the idea that he might have to look after Star Archie felt a leap of hope, then felt bad about it. Star and Ted were together again, as it should be. As casually as he could, he asked,

"Do you want me to look after him while you're away, sir?"

"I want you to – oh, you know. He's your dog, Archie."

It felt as if time had stopped. As if something miraculous had happened. But it couldn't.

"Sir—" he struggled to make sense. "Sir, you know I love Star. I'd love to have him. But he's not a thing you can give away, sir. He's yours, he just is. You're his man and he's your dog. You can't change that."

"It's already changed." Ted smiled a little sadly. "I've seen the way he greets you. And you're secure for him, Archie. You'll be staying here at Ashlings, working with your father. I don't know where I'll end up. I don't even know where I'll go and what I'll do after Norway, and whether I could take him, and whether I'll get – you know, ill again. It's not fair to him. You're the one he looks to now. He's happy with you. Chuck him a pair of my smelly old socks now and again."

Archie looked down. Star was gazing up at him, his tail wagging as if he expected something good to happen. But still, Archie's eyes stung. He had to do the right thing.

"I can't take him from you, sir," he said. "Even when we thought you were dead, he was still Master Ted's dog. He always will be."

"Walk away and whistle," said Ted. "He'll follow you. Go on."

Archie turned away, crammed his hat over his ears, turned up his collar, stuffed his hands into his pockets, and walked out at the front door of Ashlings Hall into starlight, folding his lips firmly, staying silent. He would not whistle. He turned left to walk to the cottage where Jenn and Flora would be hanging up stockings.

Ted stood at the door. Star looked up at him, waiting, hopeful, his eyes bright and his ears lifted.

"Seek him, Star," said Ted. "Seek your master." So Star jumped down the steps, ran out into the snow, and trotted home at Archie's side.